"You don't think he'll change his mind?"

"He will not. He thinks me *soiled*." The word caught in Eve's throat. "He'll have me shunned if I don't marry. But I've never even been out with a boy."

Levi returned to his pacing. "You've got a problem here."

"*Ya*, I do." Eve gave a little laugh that reflected no humor. "And it's already been a week. My father is threatening to tell our bishop tomorrow and have me shunned immediately. He'll put me out then. I know he will."

"I can only think of one alternate solution here, Eve, and you may not like it, but—"

"Anything," she whispered, "because I'm afraid if I'm forced, I might choose to marry Jemuel rather than lose myself. Lose my life. And that's what would happen if I went into the *Englischer* world. I know it." She looked up to him. "What can I do?"

Levi held her gaze and shrugged. "You can marry me."

Emma Miller lives quietly in her old farmhouse in rural Delaware. Fortunate enough to have been born into a family of strong faith, she grew up on a dairy farm, surrounded by loving parents, siblings, grandparents, aunts, uncles and cousins. Emma was educated in local schools and once taught in an Amish schoolhouse. When she's not caring for her large family, reading and writing are her favorite pastimes.

Books by Emma Miller

Love Inspired

The Amish Spinster's Courtship
The Christmas Courtship
A Summer Amish Courtship
An Amish Holiday Courtship
Courting His Amish Wife

The Amish Matchmaker

A Match for Addy
A Husband for Mari
A Beau for Katie
A Love for Leah
A Groom for Ruby
A Man for Honor

Visit the Author Profile page
at Harlequin.com for more titles.

Courting His Amish Wife

Emma Miller

LOVE INSPIRED
INSPIRATIONAL ROMANCE

LOVE INSPIRED®

INSPIRATIONAL ROMANCE

Recycling programs
for this product may
not exist in your area.

ISBN-13: 978-1-335-75867-5

Courting His Amish Wife

Copyright © 2021 by Emma Miller

This edition published by arrangement with Harlequin Books S.A.

For questions and comments about the quality of this book, please contact us
at CustomerService@Harlequin.com.

Love Inspired
22 Adelaide St. West, 40th Floor
Toronto, Ontario M5H 4E3, Canada
www.Harlequin.com

Printed in U.S.A.

And we know that all things work together for good to them that love God, to them who are the called according to his purpose.

—*Romans* 8:28

Prologue

Through the trees, Eve spotted her father's windmill and ran faster, ignoring the branches and underbrush that tore at her hair and scratched her arms and face. She took in great gulps of air, sobbing with relief as she sprinted the final distance. She had prayed to God over and over throughout the night. She had begged Him to see her home safely. Now the sun was breaking over the horizon, and she had made it the more than ten miles home in the dark.

Bursting from the edge of the woods, she hitched up her dirty and torn dress, the hem wet from the dew, and climbed over the fence. In her father's pasture, she hurried past the horses and sheep, her gaze fixed on the white farmhouse ahead. If she could just make it to the house, her father would be there. She would be safe at last, and he would know what to do.

Trying to calm her pounding heart, Eve inhaled deeply. At last, her breath was coming more evenly. She wiped at her eyes with the torn sleeve of her favorite dress. She was safe. She was home. Her father would protect her.

At the gate into the barnyard, she let herself through and slowed to a walk as she neared the back porch. Her father's beagle trotted toward her, barking in greeting. Through the windows, she could see into the kitchen where a light glowed from an oil lamp that hung over the table. Her father and sisters and brothers would be there waiting for her. As she climbed the steps to the porch, her wet sneakers squeaked. Hours ago, she had crossed a low spot in the woods and soaked her canvas shoes.

She had almost reached the door when it swung open.

"Dat," she cried, throwing herself at him, bursting into tears. "Oh, *Dat.*"

"Dochter." Her father grasped her by the shoulders, but instead of embracing her, he pushed her back. "Where have you been?" he demanded in Pennsylvania *Deitsch.* He looked her up and down, not in relief that she was safely home, but in anger. "Where is your prayer *kapp*?"

Eve raised her hand to her hair to find it uncovered. "Oh," she cried. "I must have… I must have lost it in the woods somewhere." She brushed back her brown hair that had come loose from the neat bun at the nape of her neck to fall in hanks around her face. She pulled a twig from her hair. *"Dat.* Something terrible happened. I—"

"Where have you been all night?" he boomed, becoming angrier with her by the second. "Who have you been with?" he shouted. "To sneak out of my house after I forbade you to go? I should beat you!"

When she looked up at him, Eve realized she had made a terrible mistake. It had taken her hours to find her way home. She had walked and run all night, choosing the long way home because she had been afraid to follow any main roads for fear Jemuel would find her. She had climbed fences, been scratched by briars and been chased by a feral dog. At one point, she had been lost and worried she had walked too far, or in the wrong direction. But she hadn't given up because she knew that if she could make it home safely, everything would be all right.

But looking at her father's stern face, at his long, thick gray beard and his angry eyes that stared at her from behind his wire-frame glasses, she realized she was wrong. She wasn't safe. And perhaps she would never be so again because she knew what her father was going to say before the words came out of his mouth.

He pointed an accusing finger. "You will marry that boy!" Amon Summy shouted, spittle flying from his mouth.

Eve lowered her head, tears streaming down her cheeks as she prayed fervently to God again to help her.

Chapter One

Levi snapped off a leaf of fresh mint from Alma Stolz-fus's pot of herbs near her back door and popped it into his mouth. He was standing with a group of young women, all of marrying age, all looking for husbands. *A fox in the henhouse*—that's what his grandmother would have called him. Because he was single, too.

The difference was, he wasn't here to gobble up any of these girls. He wasn't even looking for a girl to offer a ride home this evening after the singing. He intended to ask Mari, Alma Stolzfus's niece, to let him take her home, though right now, he wasn't even sure she would say yes. They were a bit on-again, off-again. One week she was bold enough to ask him to drive her home from one of the Saturday night singings, and the next she barely spoke to him.

Levi had the idea that she was more interested in JJ Yoder than him. The problem was that JJ was the quiet, reflective type. He was too shy to ask a girl to ride home with him, which was the typical way young men and women got to spend time alone together in pursuit of the right spouse. JJ certainly wasn't asking any girl out for an ice-cream cone or inviting her to his family's home on a visiting Sunday. It was Levi's theory that Mari was going out with him occasionally only to make JJ jealous enough to ask her out himself, which was okay with Levi. He liked Mari, but more as a friend. That didn't mean he wouldn't have accepted a kiss if she offered, but that was about as unlikely as her aunt Alma giving him one.

"What about you, Levi?" Trudy Yoder, JJ's sister, cut her eyes at him. She was one of the prettiest girls standing there, and she knew it. "You going to the barn raising at Mary Aaron's grandfather's tomorrow?"

He suspected Trudy was openly flirting with him, the way she was swinging her hips ever so slightly, smiling and batting her feathery eyelashes.

His hunch was confirmed when her sister harrumphed and slipped her arm through Trudy's. "Come, *Schweschder.* We'd best see if Alma needs any help getting the lemonade and snacks on the table."

Trudy resisted her sister's tug on her arm. "So are you going?" she asked Levi.

"*Ya,* I'm going to the barn raising," he answered lazily. It had been a warm day, even for the end of May, and it was supposed to be sunny, warm and clear the following day, perfect conditions for a barn raising. The work crews would show up at dawn and work until sunset. It would be a long day, but Levi enjoyed barn raisings. He liked knowing he had helped a family, and the food served, often three full meals, was always exceptional.

"You are?" Trudy was grinning again. "And is there

a kind of cookie you especially like, Levi? My *mam* and I are baking twelve dozen for the midday meal." The apples of her cheeks were as rosy as the dress she was wearing. Like the other girls, she had kicked off her shoes for the volleyball game they'd just played, boys against girls, and hadn't put them back on. She was cute and sweet, and he wondered if Mari didn't want to ride home with him if he ought to ask Trudy.

"We're making cookies, too. Peanut butter with peanut butter chips," Mary With-A-Y said. That was what they called her because she was also Mary Stolzfus, a cousin of Mari's, only she spelled her name differently. "I made some a few weeks back and took them to the Fishers' for visiting Sunday. I bet Levi ate a hundred of my cookies."

The Fishers, relations to the Fishers back home, were the folks Levi lived with. Though his home was in Hickory Grove in central Delaware, he was a buggy maker's apprentice to Jeb Fisher there in Lancaster County, Pennsylvania. Because Jeb and his wife had never been blessed with children, they opened their home to young men interested in learning to build buggies. Right now, Levi was sharing a room with Jehu Yutzy from Ohio.

"He ate a hundred of *your* cookies!" One of the other girls, whose name he didn't remember, laughed. "I bet Levi would eat *two hundred* of *my* chocolate-chocolate chip cookies. You like chocolate-chocolate chip, don't you, Levi?" She gazed up at him with big, green eyes.

Levi chewed thoughtfully on the mint leaf in his mouth, enjoying the sweet, cool flavor. "The truth is, I love all cookies," he said diplomatically. And that was a fact. He did love to eat. "You're all such good cooks around here, how could a man choose?"

The girls giggled in response and began to call out the kind of cookies they could make for Levi.

"Levi." Someone whispered in his ear from behind, and he turned, surprised because he hadn't seen her approach. It was Mari.

He smiled at her. "There you are. I was wondering where you had—"

"Sht," she shushed, speaking so softly that only he could hear her. "I need your help. It's important."

He looked into her eyes and immediately saw that something was wrong. Very wrong. He glanced at the circle of young women who looked like Englisher-dyed Easter eggs in their pastel-colored dresses of blue and pink and green. They hadn't seemed to notice Mari and were talking among themselves about the ingredients in their recipes.

He returned his gaze to Mari. "You need me now?"

"Right now."

By the tone of her voice, he guessed he wouldn't be getting a kiss. He studied her worried face, trying to figure out what was going on.

"So, are you coming or not?" Mari asked. She looked him up and down and then walked away.

Levi pushed his straw hat down farther on his head, nodded to the girls and followed Mari.

Eve sat on a bale of straw in the Stolzfuses' barn, her knees drawn up, arms wrapped around them. She stared at the toes of her water-stained, black canvas sneakers. "What am I going to do? What am I going to do?" she whispered. The phrase had become a chant over the last week. A prayer.

Where am I going to go? she wondered. *Where will I live? How will I make money to eat?*

A speckled black-and-white Dominique chicken scratched in the wood shavings at Eve's feet and clucked contently. She watched the chicken, thinking how curious it was that life around her went on without acknowledging that her life, as she knew it, was over. Of course, no one but her father and her cousin Mari knew what had happened.

And Jemuel. *He* knew.

Eve took a deep, shuddering breath. It was warm inside the enormous dairy barn and smelled comfortingly of fresh hay, straw and well-cared-for animals. A black cat leaped up onto the bale of straw and rubbed against her. Eve stroked its back, and it purred, watching the chicken.

The chicken paid no attention to the cat and wandered off, still searching for a stray morsel of corn or grain on the swept concrete floor. The cat seemed to know that things wouldn't end well if it pounced on the chicken. Alma Stolzfus wouldn't have a cat on the property that harmed any animals but a rat or a mouse.

Eve glanced up at the closed barn doors. The larger of the two, meant to lead farm stock or equipment through, had a wide crack at the top that needed caulking. The late afternoon sun poured through the opening, and she watched the movement of dust motes. The way they were illuminated in the beams of sunlight, they seemed to twinkle, reminding her of the stars in the heavens.

Was her life truly over? Her *dat* had said it was if

she didn't do as he ordered. But how could it be over?
She was only twenty-two. She had too many dreams to
have reached the end so soon. She had imagined having a handsome husband, her own home, a house full
of children. She had imagined being happy.

Would she ever find happiness now? Or at least con-
tentment?

Eve pressed her lips together, fighting tears that
brimmed in her eyes. There had to be an answer to her
dilemma. There *had* to be.

Mari had said she could help. Mari was a cousin she
didn't often see because Eve's father had had a disagreement with Mari's father, *his* cousin, many years ago.
And Eve and Mari didn't belong to the same church district, so the only time they saw each other was at young
people's social events. There were plenty of chaperoned
frolics for young men and women of marrying age in
the county, but Eve didn't get to go often because of her
responsibilities at home.

As the eldest of six children and because their mother
had died years ago, it fell to Eve to do the cooking
and cleaning and other household chores in her father's
home. Her sister Annie, at nineteen, was a great help,
but the burden of being in charge was still firmly bal-
anced on Eve's shoulders. With meals to cook, the house
to clean, laundry to do and clothes to be sewn for her
growing brothers and sisters, she didn't get out often.
That was at least partially how she'd ended up in this
situation to begin with. She didn't get to spend much
time with other young women or men, and she had
never been on a date. Not only had she never been on
a date, but a young man had never even expressed any

interest in her before. That was why, when Jemuel had paid attention to her at her father's booth at the farmers market, she'd so quickly become enamored with him.

The sound of a door opening startled Eve, and she half rose from the bale of straw she was sitting on. The standard-sized door beside the larger sliding one swung open.

"Eve, it's Mari," her cousin called as she entered the barn. "I brought someone with me. Someone who can maybe help."

"Ne," Eve said miserably, now having second thoughts about having come to the Stolzfus farm. Her father would be so angry with her if he found out she'd told someone what happened with Jemuel. The only reason he had let her come to the singing was because he had assumed she would be meeting Jemuel there to discuss their impending wedding nuptials. An assumption she hadn't corrected. She'd neither seen nor heard from Jemuel since she'd run from him, and she hoped she would never lay eyes on him again.

"I don't want anyone to know," Eve murmured. Then she saw him: Levi Miller. Though she didn't know him, she knew *of* him. Mostly because every woman in the county, ages 2 to 102, thought he was as handsome as a man could be. They had once been introduced at a girls-against-boys softball game, but it had been a year ago and she doubted he remembered her. She wasn't the kind of girl a boy remembered.

"I don't know if you've met Levi, but—"

"Ne," Eve interrupted Mari, mortified that Levi was whom she had brought. A boy? What was her cousin thinking? Did Mari really think she was going to talk

to a boy about what Jemuel had done, what he had tried to do? She twisted her fingers in the skirt fabric of her threadbare green dress. "This isn't a good idea. My father would be so angry if he found out I had told anyone. Even you," she told Mari pointedly.

"Sounds to me like he's already pretty angry." Mari turned to wave Levi, who stood in the doorway backlit by sunlight, inside. "Come in and close the door," she told him. "We don't want Trudy to know we're here. Otherwise she'll be giving her opinion."

Levi closed the door behind him. "I won't let anyone in. Not anyone you don't want here." He was speaking to Eve.

Eve waited for her eyes to adjust so she could see him and her cousin better. She imagined their eyes were adjusting, too, after coming into the barn from the bright afternoon sunshine. Which was a good thing because it gave her a moment to gather her wits. When Mari had said she might know someone who could help, Eve had assumed she meant her aunt Alma or maybe one of the other women there chaperoning the frolic. Eve would never have agreed to let Mari bring Levi Miller. What could Mari possibly be thinking to believe Eve would tell this young man anything about what had happened to her? Why would Mari think he would care?

As her eyes adjusted, there was no doubt in Eve's mind that Levi Miller was good-looking. He wasn't overly tall, but he had broad shoulders and nice hands that were clean, his nails trimmed. His hair was a medium brown, shiny and a little long, the way unmarried boys sometimes let theirs get when they were away from their mothers' watchful eyes. He had a strong chin, a long, straight nose and expressive blue-gray eyes, framed by heavy brows.

He was as handsome as she was plain.

Eve had always known she wasn't a pretty girl. But she didn't think she was ugly, either. She was just… plain. She was ordinary in looks with brown hair and brown eyes and a short, thick, round body. She was ordinary in the way a white dinner plate was ordinary. Nothing fancy, but well suited to the task. Eve's appearance was suitable to who she was: a woman of God, Amish, a big sister to three brothers and two sisters, and a daughter to Amon Summy. In that order.

"Please go." Eve lowered her gaze, unable to bear the two of them standing there looking at her.

"I don't mean to intrude," Levi said. He had a warm and steady tenor voice. "I came to see if I could help."

Eve clasped her hands together and glanced down to where the chicken had scratched in the sawdust. There were lines and shapes. As she studied them at her feet, she thought she saw a heart, and she stared at it.

A sign from God?

Eve had never been one for looking for signs from God, not like her father. He never liked to make big decisions without first praying and then waiting for a sign. When he had decided he wanted to take her out of school after she had completed the sixth grade, he had told her he would make his decision in a few days. The fact that she didn't want to quit school and stay home to work all day hadn't mattered. He had prayed and then waited for a sign. It had come in the form of a single black-eyed Susan in her mother's flower bed near the back door of their house. Her father said that was a sign from God that she was meant to be home alone during the day while the others were in school.

He had received the same sign when he decided that her sister Annie should leave school. However, their father had received no such sign from God concerning the boys in the family. Both older boys attended classes until they were sixteen, and Abiah would be in eighth grade in the fall. Eve and Annie had talked, wondering if their father would receive a sign that their sister Naomi, who had just completed the sixth grade, was to end her schooling.

"Please, Eve," Mari fretted. "I don't know how else to help you. Even though my *mam* said you might be able to stay with us for a little while, my *dat* said no. Your father and him being cousins, he said he didn't think it was right for him to get involved in a family matter. Especially since my father and yours are not on good terms."

"I can't promise you I can help, but if you don't tell me what's wrong, I know I can't," Levi said. He spoke gently to her as if she were an animal that might bolt at any moment.

"Come on." Mari sat down on the bale of straw and patted it. "Sit down and tell Levi what happened." She caught the hem of Eve's dress and tugged on it.

Eve dropped down. "You didn't tell him?"

"*Ne*, of course not. I gave you my word. I said I wouldn't tell anyone without your permission." Mari took Eve's hand in her own. "It's better if you explain to him, in your own words. It's your story to tell," she said soberly.

Eve hung her head in shame. "I can't," she whispered. How could she tell Levi Miller, the most eligible bachelor in Lancaster County, how stupid she had been? How naive?

"I wish you would." Levi walked away and came back with a milking stool. He set it an appropriate distance from the two young women and sat down, facing them. "I'm a pretty good listener. That's what my sisters say."

It took Eve a moment to find her voice. She couldn't bring herself to look at him as she spoke. "You have sisters?"

"A bunch of them. My sister Mary is older than I am and married with children. She lives in New York, where we're originally from. But my sisters back in Delaware—stepsisters technically—we talk all the time. There's Lovey, who's married and lives down the road, Ginger, who just wed in the spring to our neighbor Eli, and Bay, Nettie and Tara are still at home." He spoke slowly, his voice growing on Eve.

But Eve still couldn't look at him. It took her what seemed like an eternity to speak, but he waited patiently. She was embarrassed to tell him what had happened, but she was running out of choices. She had prayed and prayed to God to save her. What if He had sent Levi with a solution?

Eve swallowed hard, digging deep within herself to find the nerve to speak. "I did a foolish thing," she blurted.

Levi threaded his fingers together, lowering his head thoughtfully before looking up at her again. "Haven't we all?"

"*Ne*, this was *really* foolish. I didn't think it through."

Once she started to speak, she couldn't stop. It all tumbled out of her. "I met this boy named Jemuel. He's the same age as me. He seemed so nice. He came every Friday for weeks. Stopped by at my father's table at the farmers market. Jemuel and I talked, and we laughed. And one day, he brought me a turkey sandwich and an orange soda pop. He kept asking me if I wanted to go to a singing with him. I thought he was being nice, and not many boys—" Eve's voice caught in her throat.

"It's all right," Mari assured her, taking her hand again and squeezing it.

"No one ever asks to take me to a singing, or offers a ride home," Eve continued. "Not that I get to go to a lot of singings."

"Her mother passed twelve years ago, having her youngest sister. Eve cares for three brothers and two sisters, all younger. And her father. She runs the house, cooks, cleans—she does it all."

"I'm sorry to hear that. I lost my mother a few years ago. I understand how hard it is," Levi said. "Did your father not remarry?"

"He did," Eve murmured. "But she left."

They were all quiet for a moment until Mari urged, "Tell Levi what happened with Jemuel."

Eve exhaled. She was still shaky inside, but at least she didn't feel as if she was going to burst into tears at any moment anymore. "Jemuel kept inviting me out. I asked my father and asked. And every time he said no. He said he didn't know Jemuel or his family and that it wasn't—" She hesitated and then went on. "He said it wasn't safe for a young woman to ride in a buggy with a man she didn't know."

Eve was quiet long enough that Levi said, "Okay?" his tone pressing her to go on.

"I went anyway." The words came out sounding more defiant than Eve intended. "I disobeyed my father, and a week ago Friday night, I sneaked out of the house and met Jemuel at the end of our lane. We were supposed to go to a singing. I wore my favorite dress. Blue. I love a blue dress." She didn't know why she told him that detail. What did men care about what a woman wore? But she had loved that dress that was now ruined, torn in shreds, and waiting in her sewing room to become something else. The dress had reminded her of her mother because her mother's favorite color had been blue, and she had worn it all the time.

"You sneaked out of the house?" Levi pushed gently.

"*Ya.* It was after nine and dark when I left. Jemuel said the singing didn't start until later, so it would be fine going that late. I didn't use my head," she admitted. "I didn't think about the fact that singings don't start at ten o'clock at night. I was just happy that Jemuel wanted to be with me. That he liked me."

Eve took another deep breath. "So… I got into Jemuel's buggy with him. And at first, everything was fine. We were talking and laughing. He told me a funny story about chasing a calf through his sister's spinach patch. But the minute he took the beers out from under the seat, I should have been suspicious. I should have told him to turn around and take me home. Either that or I should have just gotten out of the buggy and walked home. Before it was too late." She whispered her last words.

Mari wrapped her arm around Eve's shoulders. "You're doing great. Keep going."

"I didn't drink the beer, but he did. He drank the beers and threw the cans out of the buggy. Right on the road. I didn't get suspicious, though, until I realized we were headed away from the direction where he said the singing was. But even then, I didn't make him turn around." She looked up to see Levi watching her, his face without judgment. It gave her the courage to go on.

"Instead of going to his aunt's, he drove down a long lane to an abandoned farmhouse. I told him I didn't want to go inside. That I wanted to go to the singing or home. Jemuel said we had to make a stop at the house to get something for his uncle, and then we'd go to the singing. He said the house belonged to them. He wanted me to go inside with him, and I didn't—"

Her words caught in her throat, but this time she feared she wouldn't be able to speak again.

"Take a breath," Mari encouraged, rubbing Eve's arm.

Eve inhaled deeply and went on. "I didn't want to go, but I went anyway." She spoke now in a voice barely above a whisper. She could hear the black-and-white chicken clucking in the far corner of the barn. "When we got inside, Jemuel, he...he tried to—" She felt her face grow hot and she couldn't speak.

"He tried to push himself on her," Mari finished for her.

"Push himself?" Levi didn't seem to understand what Mari was saying. Then, suddenly, the expression on his face changed. "He tried to take advantage of her," he said angrily. "Did he...harm you, Eve?"

Eve felt as if she were frozen. She couldn't speak. She couldn't move. She could barely hear. All she saw was Levi sitting there on the milk stool, handsome, smart Levi. And here she was, ugly and stupid.

"He didn't." Mari took over the explanation. "Eve hit him with a broken chair, and she ran. He chased her, but she was smart. She didn't take the road. Instead, she ran through the woods. It took her all night long, but she found her way home."

"I thought my father would go to Jemuel, to Jemuel's father, to his bishop and tell them what happened. I thought my father would defend me. I thought he would see Jemuel punished. He didn't." Tears welled in Eve's eyes. "He said it was all my fault."

"Wait." Levi came off the milk stool so quickly that he knocked it over. "Your father blamed you?" he asked, his hands on his hips as he stood before her.

Eve nodded, unable to verbally respond.

"Her father told her that she had shamed herself and the family, and the only way to make amends for her sin was to marry Jemuel," Mari finished for her.

"What sin did you commit?" Levi asked, his eyes narrowing. "Being too trusting is not a sin, Eve."

Eve pressed her lips together. "My only sin was not obeying my father, and for that, I confessed to our bishop, though I didn't tell him the details. And I apologized to my father."

"Let me make sure I have this right." Levi began to pace. "A man took you for a buggy ride, making you think he was taking you somewhere he had no intention of taking you. And then he tried to take *advantage* of you?" he asked in disbelief.

Eve hung her head.

"And if she doesn't marry Jemuel, *this week*, her father is putting her out of the house and having her shunned," Mari explained. "I tried to convince my parents to let her stay with us, but I couldn't."

"It's all right," Eve assured her cousin, smiling feebly at her. "I understand. My father can be a difficult man. I wouldn't bring those difficulties into your father's home. You don't deserve that. None of you do. But I cannot marry Jemuel," she went on, her voice so strained that she barely recognized it. "I will not. But I don't know where to go. What to do." She finally felt brave enough to meet Levi's gaze. "If I'm shunned, I'll lose everything. I've already lost my family, but to lose my God…"

"You can't lose God," Levi insisted. "No one can lose God. He's with us always."

"I'll lose everything," Eve repeated. "And I cannot lose my faith. I cannot lose my church. I know that most people our age at least consider what it would be like to leave our homes, our Amish way of life, to be an Englisher, but I never have. I love our faith, our simple ways. I love God, and I will not abandon Him." Her last words were fierce.

Mari rose, crossing her arms over her chest. "You see the problem here," she told him. "If Eve doesn't marry immediately, she's out of her father's house, out of the Amish community."

Levi nodded, still pacing. "And you don't think that your father said these things impulsively? You don't think he'll change his mind?"

"He will not. He thinks me *soiled*." The word caught

in Eve's throat. "He'll have me shunned if I don't marry. But I've never even been out with a boy. I don't know—"

The barn door opened. "Mari?"

Mari whipped around. It was one of her sisters.

"Aunt Alma is looking for you." Her sister squinted, her eyes not yet adjusted. "Who else is there with you?"

Mari rushed toward the door and grabbed her sister. "Mind your own knitting." She gave her a nudge out the door. "I'll be back as soon as I can," she called over her shoulder.

The door closed behind them, and the bright light was gone again.

"Mari's right," Levi said, returning to his pacing. "You've got a problem here."

"*Ya*, I do." Eve gave a little laugh that reflected no humor. "And it's already been a week. My father is threatening to tell our bishop tomorrow and have me shunned immediately. He'll put me out then. I know he will."

Levi stopped directly in front of Eve and looked down at her. "I can only think of one alternate solution here, Eve, and you may not like it, but—"

"Anything," she whispered, "because I'm afraid if I'm forced, I might choose to marry Jemuel rather than lose myself. Lose my life. And that's what would happen if I went into the Englisher world. I know it." She looked up to him. "What can I do?"

Levi held her gaze and shrugged. "You can marry me."

Chapter Two

Levi led his new wife through the train station lobby, a large duffel bag in each hand. He still couldn't believe he was a married man. He couldn't believe that he had impulsively asked Eve to marry him and she had said yes. Never in his wildest dreams could he have guessed he would have walked into that barn less than a week ago a single man and walked out betrothed. To a woman he didn't know.

It wasn't that he didn't want a wife. He had always seen himself someday, down the road, a happily married man like his father. But he'd seen no reason to be in a hurry to wed. His intention had been to finish his apprenticeship and return home to Hickory Grove and build buggies. He would establish a buggy shop, build and sell buggies, save money to build a home for a family and then—and only then—begin looking seriously for a wife.

And all of those carefully laid plans had vanished in a single moment.

That day in the barn when Eve told him what hap-

pened to her, his immediate impulse had been to help
her. His heart had gone out to the girl, and Levi's father had always preached to him and his siblings to help
those in need. When Eve told him she would sooner
marry the man who had tried to attack her than allow
her father to have her shunned, the idea that he could
marry her had just popped up in Levi's head. In the moment, it had seemed the perfect solution. Eve would be
able to escape her father and the awful man who had
tried to take advantage of her, and not lose her church.
Levi had known the moment he began talking to Eve
that she was a good woman, a woman of faith, the kind
he wanted to marry. What he had not considered was
what it would mean to him to marry a woman he didn't
know.

And now it was too late to reconsider. He and Eve
were wed, and marriage was forever. But he'd done
the right thing. He'd been telling himself that since he
got up this morning and lowered himself to his knees,
praying to God to show him the way to make his marriage a good one.

Levi glanced at Eve, and thoughts of himself slipped
away. She looked tired and scared, and it was his responsibility as her husband to put her at ease.

"Let's find a place to sit," Levi said. "The train won't
be here for another forty minutes, but I thought we best
be early. Early is always better than late when it comes
to catching trains and picking peaches." He chuckled
nervously at his own joke.

Eve offered a smile but said nothing.

He understood how she was feeling. The last week
had been overwhelming for him, as well.

This was the first time he and Eve had been alone since the day in the barn almost a week ago. When they parted that day, he had taken a borrowed buggy and gone directly to her father to ask for her hand in marriage. The stern-faced man had met him on the porch and not asked him to come inside, not even when Levi told him why he was there. Their conversation had been brief. Her father had been expecting the man who had tried to assault Eve. However, he had given his permission for Levi to marry his daughter anyway. Amon Summy hadn't seemed to care all that much who Levi was or why he wanted to marry Eve. Amon just wanted his daughter married and out of his home. Mari's mother had made the arrangements for her brother, the bishop in their church district, to marry the couple, and a few hours ago, Levi and Eve had wed in front of only a handful of people.

Levi had always imagined his wedding would be like the ones he had been attending since he was a child. He thought he would marry the way his father had married his stepmother and his brothers and sisters had married their spouses. He had envisioned the solemn church service and then a full day of celebration with good food, the laughter of friends and family, and generous gifts that would help him and his wife establish their new home. He'd envisioned a traditional honeymoon of traveling for a few weeks to visit relatives with his new wife before returning home to set up housekeeping.

The only thing he'd been right about was the solemn service. The sole member of Eve's immediate family who had attended had been her father, who scowled through the entire service. And while Mari and her mother and sisters had tried to make it a happy affair, not knowing the details of why they were marrying so quickly, those attempts had fallen short. They'd not even had a wedding dinner after the service. There had been no time because Levi and Eve had to get to the station to catch the train to Delaware.

"Why don't we sit here?" Levi suggested, pointing at a wooden bench in the cavernous waiting room. He glanced at Eve.

She was wearing the same green dress she had been wearing the day he met her and a dingy church Sunday apron over it. He suspected she didn't have another dress, something he would right as soon as they arrived in Hickory Grove. He was not a man of great means, but he had enough money to provide his wife's basic needs. She had brought only one small bag to Mari's that morning, a fact that he'd found slightly embarrassing because he had two large zip duffels and had made arrangements for the Fishers to bring the rest of his belongings to him the next time they came to Hickory Grove.

Levi set his bags down beside the bench and held out his hand to take the old leather case from her. There was an awkward exchange of him stepping toward her and reaching and her trying to set it down herself without touching him before he managed to take it from her. "Would you like something to drink?" he asked. "There are sodas and water in the shop. And snacks, if you're hungry."

Eve dropped down on the bench, setting her black cloak and wool bonnet on her lap. The garments were too hot to wear in the June heat and too bulky to go into a bag. "*Ne*, I'm not thirsty or hungry." She stared at the toes of her worn leather shoes poking out from beneath the hem of her dress.

Levi stood there for a minute, wanting to say something, but not knowing what. Eve looked so…so… beaten down by all the events of the last two weeks of her life that he was worried about her. She was young, only twenty-two to his twenty-nine—too young to have already been through so much. After a moment of indecision, he sat down on the bench beside her and removed his straw hat. "Eve," he said quietly. When she didn't respond, he said, "Look at me. Please?"

She slowly lifted her chin until her gaze met his. She wasn't what most would call a pretty girl, not like Mari Stolzfus or Trudy Yoder. Still, she had smooth skin that was unblemished, big, dark brown eyes framed by thick lashes and glossy hair beneath the white prayer *kapp* pinned to her head. She was shorter and rounder than a lot of girls he knew, but she was strong and healthy. And she was a woman of immense faith. Her faith was what mattered more to him because he, too, was a person of faith. So what if she wouldn't be the prettiest new bride in Hickory Grove? She was *his* bride, and the thought made him smile tenderly.

"Everything is going to be all right, Eve." His words were as much to reassure himself as her, at that moment. "You're going to like Hickory Grove. Everyone is so friendly and kind and…and they're fun. You're going to fit in so well, so easily," he told her.

She pressed her lips together, lips that were the color of the roses in his stepmother's garden. "You should call your father. It's not right to show up without warning. Your stepmother won't appreciate it. She might not want me there."

He shook his head with a smile. "You don't know Rosemary. She would welcome anyone I brought into her home, anyone that any of my brothers and sisters brought home. You're going to like her, Eve. And she's going to love you."

Eve thought on that for a moment. "And she's your *stepmother*?"

He nodded. Her question reminded him of how little they knew of each other.

"Because the way you talk about her," Eve continued, "she doesn't sound like a stepmother. My father was married a few years after my mother died, and she—she wouldn't have welcomed anyone I brought home. She didn't even want me there." Her gaze fell to her lap. "She wasn't very nice to my brothers and sisters or to me."

"You said she left." Levi fiddled with the brim of his hat. "Was that why? Did she not get along with you and your siblings?"

The slightest smile tugged at the corner of her mouth. "I guess she didn't get along well with my father, either."

He smiled at her attempt at humor.

"I don't know where she went or how she managed to leave. There was no divorce. I guess she just went home to her family in Indiana. That's where my father is from."

"Well, I didn't know your stepmother, but I'll make a wild guess that she was nothing like our Rosemary. Rosemary's going to be thrilled to have another girl in the house. She was so sad when my stepsister Ginger left home this spring to be married. Of course, we won't live with my father and Rosemary forever. We'll build our own house. My brother Joshua and his wife just moved out of the big house to live in a small house my brother Ethan was building for himself and his wife. Only Ethan ended up moving to her parents' place down the road. So there's room for us in the big house for now. I'll talk to my father about where you and I will build our place on the farm. When we're ready."

"You need to call your father," she repeated.

Levi exhaled. She was right. The truth was, he'd been putting off this phone call for days. It was going to come as a shock to his father and he'd likely be at least a little hurt that the family hadn't been invited to the wedding. But Levi had been focusing on Eve all week and trying to make everything as easy for her as possible. Having his large family or even his parents attend the wedding would only have made matters more complicated. This had been the best way to do it, he was sure. And if he was wrong, it was done.

"You're right," Levi told her. "I'll call him now, and then I'll get us some snacks for the ride."

"Do they have pay phones here?" she asked, glancing around the big, echoing waiting area of the station. "They're hard to find anymore."

"There are a few here." He started to get up from the bench, then sat down again. "Eve." When she didn't look at him or reply, he spoke her name again. "You have nothing to be nervous about. My *vader* and Rosemary and my whole family are going to adore you."

"Until they know why you married me."

"*Ne*, they're not like that. But I already told you, I

won't tell anyone. Not even my father. There's no need for anyone in Delaware to ever know."

She looked up at him, seeming so fragile that his first instinct was to put his arm around her and comfort her. He didn't, of course. It wouldn't have been proper in such a public place. Besides, they didn't know each other.

"It's not anyone's business. I married you because I wanted to." He gave her hand that was resting on the bench a quick squeeze. "Remember that. You and I stood before that bishop and before *Gott* this morning and made those vows of our free will. *Ya?*" he said softly.

Again, the hint of a smile. *"Ya,"* she repeated.

He rose again, taking his hat with him. "I'm going to go find a pay phone. I'll call my father and tell him that the driver I hired says we'll be in Hickory Grove around six. And then I'm going to buy a Coke and some spicy Doritos." He dropped his hat on his head. "You sure you don't want something?"

"Ne. Danke," she answered.

He backed away, dropping his hat onto his head. "I'll get you something anyway. Just in case." He smiled at her, showing more confidence than he was feeling. "Be right back."

Levi found the pay phones easily; he'd used them before. He'd been living in Lancaster County for almost two years and had traveled from Pennsylvania to Delaware several times. He pulled several quarters from his pocket, fed them into the phone, and then he lifted the receiver and punched in the phone number to his father's harness shop in Hickory Grove.

Levi took a deep breath as the phone rang.

"Miller's Harness Shop," came a young male voice. "How can I help you?"

Levi had expected one of Rosemary's girls to answer. They often worked in the shop, either at the cash register or in the back, doing the finer leatherwork. "Who is this?" he asked.

"Jesse Stutzman," the boy answered. "Who is this?"

It was his stepmother Rosemary's son by her first marriage. He had to be coming up on thirteen years old. Where had the time gone? When his father and Rosemary had married, Jesse had been only nine. "Jesse, it's Levi. I didn't recognize your voice. It's gotten deeper since I was last home."

"Everyone says that."

The boy sounded embarrassed, and Levi smiled to himself, remembering all too well what it was like to be thirteen. It was a trying age, no longer a child, but not yet a man.

"Is my *dat* around?"

"I just saw him walk into the back, hang on," Jesse said.

As Levi waited, he turned around. On the far side of the large, marble waiting room, he saw his wife sitting on the bench where he'd left her, still holding on to her bonnet and cloak.

"Levi?" his father said into the phone.

Levi turned his back to the waiting room. *"Dat."* The sound of his father's voice brought a tightness to his chest. It was easy, day to day, to not think about how much he missed his family, but hearing his father speak his name brought up a well of emotion. His father hadn't been keen on the idea of Levi apprenticing so far away. He preferred to have his adult children live nearby, but he had accepted the decision.

"Are you well?" his father asked in Pennsylvania *Deitsch*, the language they spoke at home.

Levi cleared his throat, responding in Pennsylvania *Deitsch*. "I'm fine."

"It's the middle of the day, *Sohn*. It's not that I don't like to hear from you, but aren't you working?" His father sounded calm; it was one of his personality traits Levi had always admired and attempted to emulate. However, his concern was still evident in his voice.

Suddenly nervous, Levi turned around again to check on Eve. She was still sitting where he'd left her, waiting for him patiently. Seeing her, the woman who was now his wife, gave him the courage he needed. "I wanted to let you know I'm on my way home. Today. Now."

"Is something wrong? Do you need me to send a driver?"

"No, nothing is wrong. I'm… We're taking the train. And I already have a driver picking us up at the Wilmington station. I'll be home by supper if there are no delays."

"You said *we*?"

Levi took a deep breath. "Eve and me. Eve is my wife, *Dat*. I'm married."

His father was quiet on the other end of the line for so long that Levi thought maybe they had been disconnected or that his father hadn't heard him. But there had been no click, no dead sound. And Levi knew his father had heard what he said because the older man had exhaled sharply.

When his father finally spoke, his voice was tight. "When did you marry?"

"This morning."

Again a pause. Then, "And you didn't think Rosemary and I would want to be there?" His tone took on a sharpness Levi rarely heard from his father. While Benjamin Miller had held high standards for his children, he had always been kind in doling out both compliments and criticism. Another trait Levi admired in his father.

"There was no time. The Fishers were there, though," he added, thinking perhaps that would somehow lessen the blow.

"Do we... Do we know the bride?"

Again, Levi looked at Eve, but this time he did not turn his back on her. He could tell his father was upset. There was no mistaking it in his tone, and Levi had the sudden desire to tell him everything that had happened to Eve and how it had turned his life upside down in only one week. But then he reminded himself of the promise he had made to Eve and a verse from somewhere in the Old Testament came to him: *A man shall leave his father and mother and hold fast to his wife.*

Levi stroked his bare chin with his hand, his chin that would never be smooth again. As a newly married man, beginning today, he would grow a beard. "You don't know her."

There was silence on his father's end of the phone again. Then, at last, he said, "I will see you when you get home, Levi."

The phone clicked, and Levi felt the backs of his

eyes sting. He blinked as he turned to the pay phone and hung up the receiver. His father had not said why he was so upset. He didn't have to. Marrying a woman suddenly, a woman his father had never met, could mean only one thing in their community. It meant that Levi had taken from a woman that which was meant only for her husband.

Levi sniffed and took a deep breath. He reached into his pocket, took out a handkerchief his stepmother had made for him and wiped his mouth. A part of him was angry that his father had leaped to such a conclusion about him so quickly. Another part was sad that his father didn't know him better. Didn't know who he had become as a man.

It hadn't occurred to Levi that when he had offered to marry Eve, his father would think what he must now think. But what else could Levi have done? Marrying Eve was the right thing to do; he knew it in his mind and deep in his heart. He wished he could explain that to his father, along with why. But he couldn't because he had made a promise, and to that, he needed to resign himself.

Pushing aside thoughts of his father, of his dismay, Levi put on a smile and went to get some snacks to share with his wife.

Accepting the hand Levi offered, Eve stepped down from the minivan that had brought them from the Wilmington train station to the little town of Hickory Grove in Kent County. She had never been to Delaware, never been anywhere outside Lancaster County, Pennsylvania, and was feeling overwhelmed. But she also felt a spark of excitement, of hope for this new life before her. A new life with Levi Miller.

Her feet on solid ground, she withdrew her hand from Levi's, clutching her wool cloak and black bonnet to her chest. Against her will, she trembled a little as she gazed up at the rambling white clapboard farmhouse. It was two stories with multiple additions, rooflines running in several directions and two red chimneys to anchor the proportions. The farmland that surrounded the house was flat with no hills and valleys like home, but beautiful in its own way. There were barns, sheds and small outbuildings galore, painted red, all dwarfed by the enormous old dairy barn that Levi had explained as they came up the driveway housed Benjamin's harness shop and the new buggy shop where he would work. Beside it had been a greenhouse that Levi's brother and stepsister ran.

Eve's gaze settled on the big home again. The house and porches were neatly painted, and blooming shrubs and a colorful assortment of flowers grew around the foundation in wide, cultivated beds. While properly plain in color and design, the house looked nothing like the dull structure with its ever-peeling paint and hard-packed dirt lawn that she had grown up in.

Levi removed their bags from the back of the van, setting them in the driveway, and then paid the driver. As the van pulled away, voices and the sound of dogs barking from inside the house caught Eve's attention.

The door to the house flew open and a large, ruddy-colored dog with only three legs bounded across the porch toward them. A woman who looked to be somewhere in her forties appeared in the doorway and held open the screen door. "Out with you," she called into the house. Another dog, almost identical to the first, also missing a rear leg, raced past the woman.

Eve watched in awe as the two dogs bounded down the porch stairs. Her father would never have allowed an animal with a disability on his property. Animals born with any disfigurement were put down at birth "for their own good," he had explained to her when she was a child. Her father had told her that a kitten with a blind eye or a pig with a clubfoot wouldn't be able to survive. Yet these full-grown dogs weren't just surviving, they were thriving. Missing a limb didn't seem to hinder their speed or frivolity one bit.

The dogs ran up to Levi, obviously recognizing him and happy to see him. "Silas and Ada," he introduced, stroking each on the head before motioning for them to sit. "My brother Jacob's dogs. Chesapeake Bay retrievers. They won't bite." He tilted his head one way and then the other. "They might lick you to death, but they won't bite."

Eve's gaze moved from the dogs to her new husband. While he appeared relaxed, the tone of his voice said otherwise. She could tell he was nervous about bringing her home with him, which made *her* nervous. What if Levi's parents wouldn't let them stay? Where would they go? Would *they* go anywhere, or would Levi send her far away to live with some distant relative? She'd heard of such things before.

"They're fine," Eve murmured. "I like dogs. Animals."

"Good, because we've got plenty of them—dogs,

cats, goats, sheep, pigs, cows, horses. Oh, and last time I was home, my brother Jesse had a pet snake."

Her eyes got round.

The corner of his mouth turned up in a half smile. "Don't worry. Rosemary wouldn't let him keep it in the house." He waved her to follow him. "Come on, meet my family."

As Levi took the stairs, a man in his fifties who looked very much like Levi, though shorter and rounder, joined the woman on the porch. This had to be her in-laws.

"*Vader*, Rosemary," Levi called. "This is Eve, my wife. Eve, my father, Benjamin, and our Rosemary."

Rosemary met Eve's gaze, and for a moment, the older woman's pretty, round face was unreadable. *What if they don't want me here?* Eve thought again.

And then Rosemary broke into a bright smile. "*Ach*, you must be tired from your travels. Come in, come in, Eve. And let me take your cloak and bonnet. It's too warm on a day like this to be holding those things." She took them from Eve's arms. "Come in and meet my daughters. They're cleaning up. We expected you for supper but figured you must have gotten held up."

"*Ya*." Eve nodded. "The train left Philadelphia late, so we arrived in Wilmington late, and then there was traffic. *Beach traffic*, Levi said?" She hadn't understood what he meant by beach traffic but hadn't asked because much of what he said she was unfamiliar with. Levi had been raised so differently than she had that she was beginning to wonder how hard it was going to be for her to transition to his way of life.

"*Ya, beach traffic*." Rosemary rolled her eyes as she

walked into the mudroom, obviously expecting Eve to
follow. "The highways get very busy in the summer because of the beaches south of here." She was hanging up
Eve's cloak and bonnet on a hook just inside the door.
"So many Englisher tourists come from Pennsylvania
and New Jersey to our beaches. But not to worry, we
know the back roads to get where we need to go without tangling with cars."

Pausing in the doorway, Eve glanced over her shoulder at Levi. He was standing in front of his father; neither was speaking. She studied the older man for a
moment. Benjamin was a sturdy, fiftyish man of medium height with rusty-brown hair streaked with gray.
He had a weathered face with a high forehead and broad
nose with a full beard that had a reddish cast, which
had also begun to gray.

The last week had been such a whirlwind that Eve
and Levi had had little time to talk. However, on the
train ride, Levi had told her about his complicated family. He said that his mother and Rosemary's husband,
Benjamin's best friend, had died six years ago. Then
Benjamin and Rosemary had wed, and both families,
except for his oldest sister, Mary, who already had a
family, had moved from New York state to Delaware
to begin anew as a *blended* family. Levi had led her to
believe that his father, Benjamin, was a kind, understanding man. A happy man.

He didn't look happy now. In fact, he seemed so un-
happy with his son that Eve was hesitant to leave Levi
alone on the porch with him.

Benjamin was speaking now. He hadn't raised his

voice, but it was obvious he was saying something Levi didn't like.

Eve wasn't sure what to do. It was her fault Levi had married without consulting his parents. Shouldn't she be at her husband's side if Benjamin was dressing him down?

Levi glanced her way. "I'll be in in a minute," he told her. "Go in with Rosemary."

Eve nodded and followed her mother-in-law through the mudroom into a big family kitchen that held not one, but two tables pushed together in an L shape. It was a kitchen nearly as big as the first floor of Eve's father's house had been.

"They're here," Rosemary announced to two young women standing at a large country-style sink doing dishes. "Eve, that's Tara." She indicated the younger of the two who Levi had told her was twenty. "And Nettie." Nettie was a little older than Eve.

In green dresses of different shades, both girls were pretty, Tara with very light red hair and Nettie with blond. Their eyes, like their mother's, were green.

Of course they were pretty, Eve thought. Everyone in this family was handsome or pretty. She was a plain wren among a flock of colorful finches, blue jays and cardinals.

"We're so glad you made it safely. I was worried something had happened, a train crash or something," Tara said, setting down a dish towel.

"Tara is a worrier," Nettie explained, rinsing off a dinner plate and setting it out for her sister to dry. "She worries so none of us have to."

"It happens," Tara threw in her sister's direction.

She turned back to Eve. "You must be starved. I made your plates. It's fried chicken, pasta salad, broccoli slaw and pickled beets. I hope you like pickled beets, *Schweschder.* Is it all right if I call you sister?" She walked toward a refrigerator, not waiting for Eve to respond. "I know I have plenty of sisters, but can you have enough?"

"You're going to love her fried chicken," Nettie put in. "Tara's the best cook in the house, after *Mam*, of course. Tara's also the chattiest. Which gets her into trouble sometimes," she added in a fake whisper.

"I don't know why you say things like that," Tara flung over her shoulder at her sister as she set the plates on the table. "*Mam* said you shouldn't tease me so much. Didn't you, *Mam*?"

"Girls, girls," Rosemary admonished.

Eve glanced in the direction of the porch, where she'd left Levi. She didn't hear any shouting from the porch. She hoped Levi's father wasn't too upset with him.

Rosemary caught her looking at the door. "He'll be in in a minute," the older woman soothed. "Sit. Relax." She smiled kindly. "You're home now."

"I can't tell you how nice it will be to have another girl in the house," Nettie said, bringing two place settings to the end of one of the tables. "Our sisters Lovey and Ginger married, and Bay is so busy with the greenhouse this time of year that I feel like all Tara and I do is cook and clean. One meal is barely over, and it's time to start preparing for the next. It will be nice to have someone else to spend time with besides Miss Worrywart."

Tara stuck her tongue out at her sister as she carried a foil-covered plate in each hand toward the table.

Nettie rolled her eyes. "Do you see what I have to deal with every day?" she asked Eve.

Eve smiled to herself. Tara reminded her of her sister Anne. She was a worrier, too, but also playful and fun. She used to stick her tongue out at Eve when their father wasn't looking.

Thinking of her sister brought a lump to her throat. She hadn't been gone even a whole day and she already missed Anne.

"Please, Eve. Sit down. Can I get you some water?" Tara asked.

The loud sound of footfalls and little boys laughing came from the hall and then filled the kitchen as twin toddlers burst into the room. They were followed by an older boy who Eve thought might be Jesse, Rosemary's son from her previous husband. The family was so big, and it was confusing as to who were Benjamin's children and who were Rosemary's. The twin boys, she knew, were Benjamin and Rosemary's. Levi had said that it had been a bit of a surprise to the family that Rosemary had given birth at her age, but the little boys had found their way into everyone's hearts and sealed the union of the two families.

Rosemary made another round of introductions, and then another sister walked into the kitchen—Bay, the one who had the greenhouse. Then Levi's brother Joshua arrived with his family, and the kitchen was so loud, with everyone talking at once, that Eve started to feel overwhelmed again. More handsome, beautiful people who seemed so content. How would she ever fit into this big, happy family?

What had she done in marrying Levi, a stranger?

When Levi walked inside with his father, Eve could tell he was upset. Levi sat down beside her to eat his supper, and everyone joined them at the table for dessert, diving into fresh strawberry pies Tara had made. Everyone was talking to Eve, asking questions, but no one, she realized, was speaking to Levi. He ate in silence, not looking up from his plate.

Was he angry with her? Eve began to wonder.

Thankfully, once she and Levi had eaten their supper and declined the pie, the family began to scatter. Nettie and Tara excused themselves to put the twins to bed, Joshua and his family went home, and the others went their separate ways to finish chores and prepare for the next day.

Eve insisted on washing Levi's dinner dishes and her own. When she took up a clean dish towel to begin drying, Rosemary told her to put it down.

"Let the dishes sit on the drainboard until tomorrow," Rosemary said. "Jesse took your bags up to your room. I know it's been a very long day for you. You turn in." She looked at Levi, who was just standing at the end of one of the tables. "I've prepared Joshua and Phoebe's old room for you."

"Thank you, Rosemary," Levi said, then looked to Eve. "Come on. It's this way."

Eve said good-night to Rosemary, the only one left in the kitchen, and climbed the stairs behind Levi. At the landing, they went down a long hall and then a second one. He opened the very last door on the right and stepped back to let her pass.

Only when Levi walked into the bedroom and closed the door behind him did Eve realize the full extent of her impulsive decision to marry a stranger. She stared at the only bed in the room, made up with a colorful log cabin patterned quilt.

She was married to Levi now.

And that meant she would share a bed with him.

Suddenly, she was afraid. And angry. Hot tears burned the backs of her eyelids. How could her father have forced her to make the choice between marrying a complete stranger and a would-be rapist?

And how had she been so foolish as to have put herself in such a position in the first place?

Chapter Three

Levi closed the bedroom door and leaned against it, his hands tucked behind him. He took a deep breath, suddenly so tired, he could barely think. He was trying hard not to second-guess his decision to marry Eve because what was done was done.

The exchange between him and his father had been worse than he had anticipated. He had suspected from the conversation on the phone back in Lancaster that his father was upset with him, but never in his life had the man he looked up to expressed such disappointment in him. Not even the time Levi had convinced his twin brothers, Jacob and Joshua, to jump out the second-story window of their barn back in New York. The twins had only been ten, he had been thirteen, and Jacob had ended up with a trip to the emergency department with a broken arm. Their father had expressed his disappointment in Levi's choices right before he assigned all of Jacob's chores to him for two months while his little brother's bone mended. But that had not been half as bad as what had happened on their porch that evening.

Levi closed his eyes, thinking back to the conversation. He'd been the one to speak up first.

"Thank you for letting me bring my wife home, *Dat*," he had said.

His father had slid his hands into his pockets and gazed out at their orchard before returning his attention to Levi. "You will always be welcome in my home, *Sohn*." His voice then cracked with emotion. "You know that. No matter what you have done."

Levi had had to bite down on his lower lip until he tasted blood to keep from shouting, "But I didn't do anything wrong, *Dadi*. I did the right thing!"

But, of course, he hadn't been able to say that because he was a man of his word. Instead, he had just stood there and listened to his father talk about the choices a man made in life and the consequences until Joshua, carrying his new baby, and his wife and young son had come walking across the yard. Then Levi's father had gone into the house.

"There's just one bed," Eve said, her voice bringing Levi back to the present.

He looked up. "What?"

"The bed." Eve's voice had taken on a tone of annoyance. She was talking quickly, her voice higher pitched than he had heard before. "There's only one bed. I can't… I won't—" She pointed, lowering her voice. "If you think I'm sleeping in that bed with you…" She crossed her arms over her chest, moisture in the corners of her eyes. "You've got another thing coming, Levi Miller!"

Levi was so surprised by the tone she had taken with him that he didn't understand what she was so upset about. And then he did. They were married. It was customary for a married couple to share a bed and procreate as God intended. She was worried he expected her to have relations with him.

He drew back, staring at her. As with his father, he was hurt, but angry, too. How could Eve think he was that kind of man? The kind of man Levi had just saved her from? He had sacrificed his father's opinion to protect her from Jemuel Yoder, and now she was accusing him of being cut from the same cloth?

"Eve, I don't expect us to sleep together," Levi snapped back. "Why would you think that?"

"That's why." She pointed at the bed again.

"But this is the room Rosemary gave us," he said defensively. "You think I should tell her it's not acceptable when she's welcomed us into her home with open arms? What will she think if I say we need separate rooms?"

Eve stared at him, a challenge in her dark brown eyes, which surprised him. In the week he'd known her, she had seemed so agreeable and thankful for his intervention. She had been so easy to please. And now she was making demands on him and causing him stress he didn't need piled on his shoulders on top of his father's disappointment in him.

Levi exhaled loudly, stepped around her, grabbed the quilt and a pillow off the bed and tossed them on the floor. Then he picked one of his bags from where Jesse had left it and strode to the door. "I'll go into the bathroom first. You put your nightclothes on while I'm gone. When I come back, you can take your turn in the bathroom. I'll sleep here on the floor." He pushed the pillow with the toe of his boot. "Will that work?"

Eve looked like she was about to burst into angry tears. Or throw something at him. Maybe both.

She gave a quick nod.

"Fine." He walked out the door, closing it behind him. The moment he was in the hall, he regretted the harshness in his voice. It didn't matter that she had spoken unkindly to him first. He knew better. His parents had raised him better. Eve was under stressful circumstances, too, and he should have kept that in mind. In fact, her situation was worse than his because she hadn't asked for any of this. *He* had offered to marry *her*. And now he was the head of their family and *he* was the one who had to take the lead in such matters. It was his duty to promote harmony in their married life.

As Levi walked down the hall, he made up his mind that he would apologize to Eve when he returned to their room. However, after preparing for bed, he returned to their bedroom to find her tucked into bed, sound asleep.

Settling onto a makeshift bed on the hard floor, Levi clasped his hands together and prayed to God to help him be a good husband to Eve. And then, exhausted, he fell asleep.

Eve woke to the heat of early morning sunlight on her face and the sound of someone moving around the bedroom. When she opened her eyes, she saw Levi, fully dressed in denim pants, a faded blue shirt and suspenders, his shaggy hair wet. He was unpacking his bags, placing items of clothing in the drawers. For a moment she watched him, then softly greeted him. *"Guder mariye."*

He turned to her, his face solemn. "I'm sorry if I woke you. Good morning."

She sat up, pressing her lips together. They'd not spoken since the night before after she'd been so terrible to him. After he walked out of their bedroom, Eve had quickly put on her nightgown, rehearsing her apology to him for when he returned. Once in bed, she said her prayers and then waited for him. But she must have fallen asleep before he returned. And now here they were, their second day of marriage.

She started to say she was sorry, but he spoke at the same time. Then both of them went silent.

"You first," she said.

He closed a drawer behind him and approached the bed. "I want to apologize for how I spoke to you last night, Eve. It's not an excuse, but I was tired and frustrated with my father and—" He looked out a big window that faced south, then back at her. "I took it out on you."

She gave a little sigh of relief, glad he wasn't angry with her. She felt so alone right now. She had no one but Levi, and she couldn't bear the thought of him being mad at her. "I wanted to tell you I was sorry, too." She clutched the bedsheet to her chest. "You didn't deserve what I said. How I said it. I was tired, too. And everything is so different here from home that I was feeling a bit…overwhelmed. Also not an excuse," she added.

He sat down on the edge of the bed beside her. "I should have brought up the subject of sleeping arrangements before we came upstairs." His blue-gray eyes were kind. "I had to accept whatever room Rosemary gave us because no one here knows that our marriage is anything different from any other marriage in my family. They don't realize we don't know each other very well."

She looked down, appreciating how delicately he was discussing the matter.

"Eve, I have no problem sleeping on the floor, but no one can know, otherwise they'll ask questions." He paused and then went on. "The same goes for how we speak to each other in front of everyone, how we are with each other. We're supposed to be newlyweds. Do you understand what I mean?"

She nodded. "You're saying we have to…act like we like each other." She lifted her chin, sneaking a peek at him when he didn't say anything. She noticed that he had not shaved except above his upper lip. Because he was married, he was now growing a beard. Which meant this was all real. She was married, and now she was Levi Miller's wife. She wasn't Eve Summy any longer, she was Eve Miller.

She met his gaze to see that he was smiling at her.

"Eve, it's not that I don't like you. What would make you say that?" he asked. "I'm just saying that we need to give the appearance of a newly married couple who, you know, planned to wed." He sat there for a moment and then pressed his hands to the tops of his legs and stood. "I'm going to go downstairs to the kitchen. You come down when you're ready."

"Ach," she said, copying the expression she'd heard her mother-in-law make the evening before. She threw

off her sheet. "I should be in the kitchen, helping Rosemary and your sisters with breakfast."

He rested his hand on the doorknob and looked back at her. "I'm sure they'll appreciate your help but take your time. They know you had a long day yesterday. I'm going to go out to the barn and give my brothers some help with feeding, and I'll see you for breakfast." He offered a smile, and then he was gone.

The minute the door closed behind him, she jumped out of bed and made it, using the pillow and the quilt that Levi had left on the floor. Then she put on the same green dress she'd worn the day before. It was her only dress now. She'd ruined the blue one two weeks ago running from Jemuel. The only other dress she had owned was the black one she wore to church, but her father had refused to let her pack it, saying it was his property. Thankfully, he had allowed her to keep the only prayer *kapp* she owned. After brushing and tying back her hair, she lovingly placed the starched white *kapp* over her hair and took great care to pin it down without mussing it. As with most Amish women, for Eve, the head covering was a symbol of her faith. It made her feel safe.

With the *kapp* set properly on her head, she took one last look at the small mirror over the chest of drawers where Levi had placed his things. Looking back at her, she saw the same brown-haired, brown-eyed wren of a girl whom she had seen in her father's home. But there was one difference, she reminded herself. She was no longer a girl; she was a married woman. She was Levi's wife. And she wanted to be the best wife she could be to him, the wife she knew she could be to such a good man. And that started today.

Despite Eve's intentions, once she was downstairs, her confidence wavered. She didn't know how it was possible, but the kitchen was even more hectic than it had been the night before. This morning not only were the family members who lived in the house there, but also his married siblings. The kitchen was full of men and women, all talking at once, talking over each other. With the women putting breakfast on the two kitchen tables, the men came in from outside, laughing and joking, giving each other heavy-handed nudges.

And there were children everywhere, more than just Rosemary and Benjamin's young ones. The children climbed over benches and ran in and out of the kitchen, squealing with laughter. One of Levi's little twin brothers Eve had met the night before chased a snow-white fluffy cat under the table and then back out. Tara, carrying a huge platter of freshly made pancakes, held the dish high as the other twin ducked under it.

"How can I help?" Eve asked Tara from the doorway.

"Oh, everything's ready. Sit down. And be sure to save a seat next to you for Levi." Tara giggled.

"Phillip," called one of the women Eve didn't know as she ducked her head under one of the tables. "Come out of there right now or I'm coming under." The young woman had to be one of the sisters. She had Tara's green eyes, and she was beautiful, with flaxen blond hair. She looked up. "Good morning, Eve. I'm Ginger." She smiled and pointed across the room. "The redhead is my husband, Eli. Eli!" she shouted. "Say hello to Levi's Eve."

In stocking feet, a red-haired man waved from the far side of the room. "Good morning, Eve. Welcome to Hickory Grove!"

"And somewhere around here is our daughter, Lizzy, and our sons Andrew and Simon," Ginger went on. "And under this table—" she ducked to look under again and then popped her head back up "—is our son Phillip, who will be washing dishes for a week if he doesn't come out from under his *grossmama*'s table." She threw her last few words in the direction of the boy's hiding place.

"*Ach*, could you put this sausage on the table?" Tara pushed a large round plate of sausage patties into each of Eve's hands. "The egg casserole is going to overcook if I don't get it out of the oven."

Eve had taken only two steps when Philip darted out from under the table right in front of her. Startled, she swayed to keep from stepping on him, and one of the plates began to tilt. "Oh no," she cried as the sizzling patties began to slide off the edge.

A blonde woman with brown eyes snatched up one of the plates off the table and caught three of the four patties midair. "Got 'em!" The fourth hit the table and shot out into the room.

Quick as a rabbit, a boy who looked to be a brother to little Phillip snatched the sausage off the floor. "Can I eat it, Abigail?" he asked, already bringing it toward his mouth.

Abigail cut her eyes at Ginger.

"*Ya*, why not?" Ginger answered with a shrug. "I'm sure he's eaten worse."

"Boys," the blonde agreed with amusement, then she

returned her attention to Eve as she set the plate on the table. "I'm Abigail. My husband is the handsome one over there." She pointed toward one of Levi's brothers standing in the mudroom doorway. She put out her hands. "Here, let me take that."

Eve gladly passed the platter to Abigail and watched as she slid the sausages she'd caught from the plate back onto the platter before setting it down.

"Ethan, right?" Eve asked. On the train, Levi had gone through his family members' names and if they were married, along with their spouses' names, but there were so many of them. She feared she'd never learn them all. "The schoolteacher?"

"That's right. We live down the road with my parents. Our son, Jaimie, is around here somewhere. Up to mischief, I'm sure."

"Let's eat," Rosemary announced loudly above the din. Then she came up behind Eve and murmured, "Don't worry. You'll get used to the hubbub when everyone is here. They were all so eager to meet you that I couldn't tell them they weren't welcome to join us for breakfast."

She said it so kindly that Eve glanced up appreciatively. Rosemary was smiling at her and she smiled back.

"Go on, join your husband," Rosemary told her, indicating an empty seat on one of the benches beside where Levi sat. "We don't sit in any particular order around here. It's wherever you can find a place. Except for the head of the table." She pointed.

Eve looked over to see Benjamin taking a chair at the end of one of the tables.

"Makes him think he's in charge," Rosemary whispered in her ear.

Eve looked up and giggled, and Rosemary squeezed her hand, offering another kind smile. "We really are glad to have you here," she said quietly. "Now go on, before someone else takes your seat and you're stuck eating with the little ones." She looked up. "Not there, Jaimie," she ordered. "That's Eve's seat. Come over here with your *grossmammi*, where I can keep an eye on you."

After the entire family was seated and had silent grace, everyone began talking again, firing questions at Eve. As they talked across the tables, holding multiple conversations at once, they passed around serving platters of fluffy egg-and-cheese casserole, sausage, bacon, toast, hash browns and dried apple muffins. As Eve ate, she tried to answer questions posed to her as best she could and keep up with as many conversations at once as she could manage. And she listened for names, trying to keep everyone straight, making notes to herself of questions she had for Levi later. She had so many.

How did Ginger and Eli have four children if they'd just married? Why did Marshall, Benjamin's eldest son, and Abigail live with her parents rather than on the family farm? And who was Benjamin calling Rosebud?

It wasn't until after breakfast that Eve realized how quiet Levi had been through the entire meal, and how little anyone had said to him. As he rose from the table, she got up, too. All of the men were pushing back from the table and making their way out the back to go about their day. As was customary, the women would clean up. Eve didn't mind at all, though. She had known

Levi's family less than a day, but she already knew she wanted to be a part of it. Contributing to the day-to-day running of the household was a way she felt she could do that.

Eve scooped up several dirty plates and was walking toward the sink when she caught Rosemary watching Levi. The older woman glanced at Eve, then at Levi again. "Levi, did you forget something?" the older woman said.

"Sorry?" He turned to his stepmother.

"Aren't you forgetting something?" She gestured to Eve.

Eve pulled the dirty plates closer, feeling her cheeks grow warm. She didn't like being the center of attention, especially in this big, lively family.

Levi stared blankly at Rosemary.

"Your wife," his stepmother said. "You didn't say goodbye to your new wife."

Embarrassment showed on Levi's face and Eve felt awful for being the cause. "*Ne*, it's…all right," Eve said. "He… He has work to do."

"Nonsense. Today is your first full day as a married couple," Rosemary lectured. "Habits you start now, you'll carry the rest of your days." She eyed Levi again as she took the pile of dishes from Eve. "Your father would never leave the house without telling me goodbye, Levi."

He looked down at the floor.

"Go on," Rosemary urged Eve. "Spend a moment with your husband. It will be hours before he's back for the midday meal, which we eat at one. This time of year, supper is at six thirty."

Not knowing what else to do, Eve met Levi halfway.

"I'm sorry," she mouthed, looking up at him. She twisted her fingers together in the folds of her apron.

"Not your fault," he told her, his tone measured. "I'm going to help Jacob with a problem with one of the plows, then meet with my *dat* so we can discuss plans to expand the size of what will become my buggy shop, and I'll see you for dinner." Their heads together, he spoke softly so no one else in the kitchen could hear them. "Will you be all right here with Rosemary and the girls?"

Eve studied Levi's stubbled face. This morning, Abigail had called her husband handsome, but Eve thought maybe the brother she had married was even better-looking. She smiled at him. "*Ya*, of course. I'll be fine. I'll help with the dishes and then I'm sure there's other work to be done."

Tara, who was walking by them with two dirty glasses in each hand, thrust her head between Levi's and Eve's. "Don't worry, Levi. I'll be here. I'm going to make strawberry jam. Do you like making jam, Eve?" She beamed. "I love making jam."

"I do," Eve answered.

"Thank you, Tara." Levi clapped his hand on his sister's shoulder and walked out of the house.

Eve immediately went back to clearing off the table, quickly finding the rhythm of Rosemary and her daughters who still lived at home. Lovey, who was obviously expecting, and her husband, Marshall, and son, Elijah, had said their goodbyes, as had Phoebe and Joshua and their two little ones. Abigail and her family had been the first to go. From what Eve had been able to gather, Abigail's mother was poorly and she needed to get home to her. Eve would ask Levi later about Abigail's mother's health.

Eve was gathering another stack of dirty dishes when Bay, Ginger's twin sister, called from the sink, "Want to wash, Eve?"

"*Ya*, I'll wash." Eve lowered the dishes into the dishwater. "I don't mind."

Bay looked to her mother, who was helping one of the twin boys get his socks on so he could go with his father to the barn. James—at least Eve thought it was James—lay on his back, his bare feet in the air. Rosemary was trying to slip on the sock, but the little boy was wiggling.

"*Mam*, Eve's going to wash dishes. May I go? I have marigold seedlings to transplant before it gets too warm." Bay was already backing away from the sink to give Eve room. *"Mam?"*

Finally, wrestling the second sock on her son's foot, Rosemary glanced up. "Go, go," she shooed.

Bay rushed to the laundry room to make her way outside, whipping off her everyday apron. *"Danke!"*

"You're going to forget how to do household chores," Rosemary called after her daughter. "Then what will you do when you're married?"

"I don't know, maybe I won't marry at all." Bay poked her head back into the kitchen. "Or maybe my husband will do the housework and I'll support us running the greenhouse."

Rosemary frowned as she helped the little boy, who she realized was Josiah, not James, to his feet. "I wouldn't count on that, *Dochter*."

The door closed loudly behind Bay, and Rosemary rolled her eyes. "That one." She gave her son a nudge. "Go on with you. Your *dat* is waiting for you on the porch."

The little boy took off, and Rosemary turned back to Eve. "If you're going to make strawberry jam today, Eve, you best change into a different dress."

Eve thrust her hands into the warm, soapy water and began to scrub a plate with a dish brush. "This is all I have," she said softly, embarrassed.

"Oh," Tara said, stopping in the middle of the floor. She had been flitting around in the kitchen like a little bee since Eve had come downstairs this morning, but now the bee was very still. Tara was thinking. "Well then, you could have a couple of my dresses." She shrugged cheerfully. "I have too many anyway."

Eve could feel Rosemary watching her, even though her back was to the older woman. "I, uh…" Eve rinsed the plate in her hands. "I don't think it would fit," she managed.

"Well, why wouldn't it fit?" Tara set her hands on her hips. "Is it because you're too—"

"Too long," Rosemary interrupted. "Your dresses would be too long for Eve."

Eve didn't realize she had been holding her breath until she exhaled. And whispered a prayer of thanks to God for steering Rosemary to such a tactful explanation. Though it had to be obvious, she thought. Tara was much thinner and taller than Eve.

"Which means," Rosemary continued, bringing her hands together, "you and I, Eve, need to meet in my sewing room once this kitchen is *ret* up. I have a lot of extra fabric. I'm going to make you a dress."

"Oh, no. You don't need to do that," Eve said.

"*Ne*, I don't. But I want to so I don't want to hear another word about it," Rosemary said as she took a dish towel from a drawer and began to dry the clean dishes Eve was setting on the sideboard.

"But Eve and I are making strawberry jam," Tara protested.

"Not until you've picked the strawberries," Rosemary chastised.

And that was that.

Chapter Four

Levi lifted a couple of two-by-fours from the wagon onto his shoulder and carried them through an open bay door, sidestepping one of Jacob's dogs. "One way or the other, Ada," he muttered, walking out of the bright sunshine into the barn's shade.

When his family had moved to Hickory Grove from New York after his father married Rosemary, the two-story structure with a gambrel roof had been a dairy barn. His father had cleverly added interior walls to build a storefront for his harness shop, and several more rooms to create workspaces for the harness business that was their family's livelihood. Once they were settled in, and the shop had begun to thrive, the older man had built himself a small workshop for what had started out as a hobby but was becoming a passion. Benjamin Miller had always dreamed of building buggies, like his grandfather. The previous Christmas, Levi and his father had talked about adding space and bay doors to the buggy shop when Levi completed his apprenticeship and returned home. Now with Levi home to stay, the plans were being moved up, and construction on additional walls had begun.

Jacob followed behind Levi, carrying more lumber. Their father had put Jacob, a carpenter by trade, in charge of constructing the framework of the walls. Even though Levi had plenty of experience building interior walls, he was just his brother's assistant.

"Ada," Jacob called, steadying the boards on his shoulder to point into the barnyard with his free hand. "Get out from under our feet. Go chase a rabbit or something." The Chesapeake Bay retriever took off running, and he shook his head as he lowered the wood to the stack Levi had started. "Phew, going to be another warm one."

Setting down the wood he had carried inside, Levi removed a handkerchief from his pocket. He lifted his straw hat and wiped his brow, saying nothing. He had too much on his mind for small talk. Right now, he wanted to get the wagon of lumber unloaded and un-hitch the horse because the sooner these walls went up, the sooner he could get to the business of building his first buggy. With the proceeds, he would be able to open a bank account to begin saving for the house he would build on his father's property for him and Eve to live in.

"But better than rain, though, *ya*?" Jacob asked, removing his hat and fanning himself with it.

An orange barn cat rubbed against Levi's ankle, and he pushed it away gently with his boot, hoping it got the message. He didn't recognize the half-grown calico; it was probably one of his brother's rescues. Jacob loved animals and was always bringing strays home. He took a particular liking to the sick and injured. Back in Up-

state New York, his younger brother had once rescued
a litter of kittens from a tree's hollow after a neighbor's
mother cat had been killed on the road. Jacob had insisted their mother let him keep the newborn kittens in
the kitchen in a cardboard box where he had fed them
cow's milk from a tiny bottle for weeks. Every single
kitten had survived.

"You know what's for dinner?" Jacob leaned down
to pet the cat Levi had shooed away. "Seems like breakfast was a long time ago. I'm starving."

"I don't know what we're having." Levi hooked his
thumb in the direction of the bay door. "Let's get the
rest of this wood unloaded. I'd like to see some progress on these walls today."

Levi started for the door, but Jacob stepped sideways, blocking his way.

"What's going on with you?" Jacob asked.

"What do you mean?" Levi didn't meet his gaze as
he slid his handkerchief back into his pocket. "We need
to get the rest of the wood so I can put the wagon away
and unhitch the horse. Sassafras is old. No need to let
her stand out in the sun." He set his hat on his head.

Jacob studied him for a moment, making Levi uncomfortable.

"*Ne*, it's more than that." Jacob studied him. "You
don't seem like yourself. You seem…frustrated."

"That's because I *am* frustrated." Levi threw out his
arms. "I came home to get this business off the ground.
To build buggies. I have the skill, the knowledge, and
Dat's got me mending fences, hauling wood and—and
framing walls." He swung one hand in the direction of
the empty space.

The old mare they'd brought from New York lifted its head, gazing in Levi's direction when he raised his voice. Even their old horse was upset with him, Levi thought morosely.

"Come on. You've been home less than a week," Jacob argued, his tone calm. "And if we're going to make more space for you to build those buggies, we have to put up walls. *Dat*'s already moved up his plans by a good six months so you can start working."

Levi crossed his arms over his chest and said nothing. Tomorrow he'd have been back in Hickory Grove a week. He'd have been married a week, and still, his father was upset with him. And things weren't going much better with his wife.

Levi didn't see much of Eve during the day. She worked in the kitchen and in the garden with Rosemary and the girls, and Levi did what his father asked of him around the farm. They had meals together, of course, but then they were in a room full of people. Only at night were he and Eve alone and then, the moment Levi closed the bedroom door, both of them became irritable with each other. She seemed upset with him the minute she got within six feet of him, and he responded with equal, irrational crossness. He hadn't thought it would be easy to be a new husband under the circumstances, but this wasn't what he had expected at all. Not from Eve and, worse, not from himself.

"You need to have patience," Jacob urged gently. "You know how *Dat* is. He likes things to go as planned and when they don't…" He shrugged. "It takes him a little time to adjust."

"Are you talking about me wanting to start the business sooner, or my marriage?" Levi asked.

"Both."

Levi looked away. He respected Jacob's honesty with him. He watched the orange cat trot across a two-by-four they'd added to the pile, comically trying to balance as the board tilted under its weight. "*Dat* is disappointed in me," he said quietly.

"He loves you, Levi. You just need to give him some time."

Levi nodded, appreciating the fact that his brother didn't go into the specific reason why his father was disappointed in him. "I know," he murmured. "But I want to get to work. I have to build a buggy so I can sell it, so I can have some money to start saving for a house for Eve and me. So we can get out of *Dat*'s house."

"Right. You're a married man now, aren't you?" Jacob smiled good-naturedly. "How are you finding that so far?"

Levi sighed. "Honestly?" He met his brother's gaze. Jacob had their father's brown eyes. "Not what I expected. It's…harder than I thought it would be. I'm not sure what Eve wants from me."

"Well…" He drew in a breath slowly. "I imagine Eve could use a helping of your patience, too. From what she had to say about her family life, Hickory Grove has to be quite a change." He chuckled. "This family has to be a whole lot different from what she's used to."

Levi responded testily. "How do *you* know what she came from?"

"Because I asked her," Jacob pushed back.

Levi set his jaw, surprised by the jealousy that flared

in his chest. "When were you conversing with my wife? Where was I?"

"We were in the garden this morning. You'd gone to the lumberyard, and Tara asked me to help her and Eve with the pole beans' trellises. One of the wooden posts was leaning, and the wires had loosened up." He shrugged. "We talked while we worked. She seems very nice, your wife. I like her."

"I bet you do."

Jacob frowned. "What's that supposed to mean?"

Levi walked away from his brother and into the bright sunlight without another word.

Eve picked up a stack of white bowls from the kitchen table, then set them down again, flustered, not recalling what Tara had just told her. "Should I take the bowls outside now or wait?"

Tara closed the freezer door, wiping her hands on her apron. "You should leave them. We're going to go outside and sit for a while. Then we'll have the strawberry ice cream when the men get back from the barn. No telling how long they'll be. You know how men are." She brought the fingers of one hand to her thumb repeatedly. "Talk, talk, talk. *Mam* says women have nothing over men when it comes to gabbing on a visiting Sunday."

"I don't know. Maybe I should stay here." Eve gazed around the large, airy kitchen. "And get things ready."

"*Ne*. Everything is already set. Ice cream is in the freezer. Bowls and spoons are out." Tara grabbed Eve's hand. "I want you to get to know my new friend Chloe. She just moved here with her aunt and uncle from Indiana." She halted in the laundry room, turning to Eve, her eyes wide. "Did I tell you she was betrothed, but she broke it off? I don't know why. No one does, but I'm hoping once we're better friends, she'll tell me."

Eve hesitated before she spoke, considering whether it was best to keep her thoughts to herself. That had always been her father's advice. He used to tell her that no one wanted to know what she thought about anything. But it seemed to her that in Levi's family, opinions, as well as discussion, were welcome, even encouraged. And she so wanted to be a part of this family, to be one of them. She wanted to be a good wife and a good sister-in-law and daughter-in-law.

"Tara," Eve said gently, pulling her hand from hers. "It might be that Chloe doesn't want to share what happened between her and her betrothed."

Tara blinked her pretty green eyes. "Why?"

Eve shrugged, thinking of her own circumstances that brought her to Hickory Grove. "Maybe it's painful for her."

Tara seemed to consider that for a moment, and then her jaw dropped. "Oh. *Ya*, maybe you're right. I wouldn't want to upset her." She seemed a bit disappointed. "So you *don't* think I should ask her?"

Eve shook her head. "Definitely not. If she wants to tell you once you know each other better, she will."

"You're probably right." Tara gave Eve a quick hug. "Thank you."

Eve hugged her back. "For what?"

"For keeping me out of hot water with my *mam*. She's always saying my mouth gets me in trouble." She shrugged. "And for being my friend. For being my sister. *Mam* says that when you love someone, you have to tell them when they're about to make a mistake. Even if you might hurt their feelings. But don't worry. My feelings aren't hurt."

Eve bit down on her lower lip. Since her arrival, everyone in Levi's family had been kind to her, but Tara had gone out of her way to include Eve in her everyday life, offering friendship at every turn. This first week of marriage had been so hard for Eve that she didn't know what she would have done without Tara.

So far, marriage was not at all what she had imagined it would be. Of course, when she had thought about marrying when she was younger, it had been in only a dreamy sort of way. She'd assumed she would get to know her betrothed before their wedding day, courting for months, maybe even a full year. She thought she would know the man she married as well as she knew herself before they set up housekeeping together.

The truth was, she didn't know Levi at all. She knew that he was a good man, of course, a man of faith. She knew he was kind; else, he would never have offered to marry her. But she didn't know who he was as a person much beyond his devotion to his family—his father in particular—and his love for food. They'd barely talked in the week between his proposal and the wedding. Then once they arrived in Hickory Grove, they spent most hours of the day apart.

The only time they were alone was in the bedroom they shared, and that was quickly becoming a disaster. By the time they climbed the stairs to bed, they were both spent from a day of hard work. The forced closeness before they knew each other put them both on edge, and Eve found she could barely tolerate Levi once he closed their bedroom door. He was so handsome and such a catch that Eve felt unattractive and undeserving of him. And she took it out on him.

The night before, she had gotten up in the middle of the night to use the bathroom and accidentally tripped over his foot where he lay on the floor. When he cried out in pain, startled from his sleep, she'd been cross with him, telling him it was his fault. Levi's behavior hadn't been much better. Two nights before, she'd opened the window because she was hot. Then he'd closed it, saying he was cold on the floor. Still hot, she'd opened it again, only for Levi to get up and slam the window shut so hard that the glass had rattled and Rosemary had called from the end of the hallway, asking if everything was all right.

Eve knew this was not how a man and woman, bound by marriage, were supposed to treat each other, but she didn't know what to do about it. And she had no one to ask because no one in Hickory Grove, including Levi's family, knew them to be anything but a happily married couple.

"Want to go talk to Chloe until the men come back from the barn?" Tara asked, stealing Eve from her reverie.

Eve found a brave smile, thankful for the friendship Tara had offered so readily. "*Ya*, let's."

Hand in hand, they went out of the house and into the backyard. There, women sat in the shade of giant maple trees, small children played in the grass and babes slept in their mothers' arms.

Because it was visiting Sunday and there was no church for their district, Rosemary had taken the opportunity to invite friends over. According to Tara, her family either had friends and family over or went visiting every Sunday that they didn't attend services. While there were no church services on visiting day, it was still meant to be a day of rest. Any unnecessary work was frowned upon. The men fed and watered the animals, but no one hitched a plow or repaired a shutter. The women provided meals, but there was no scrubbing of floors or picking strawberries. Meals were simple: either foods like soups and casseroles were prepared the day before and reheated on the back of the woodstove, or they ate sandwiches or cold salads, also prepared before the Sabbath.

Benjamin, like Eve's father, had gathered his family in their parlor for morning and evening prayers, but there ended the similarity between Eve's old visiting Sunday and her new one. Benjamin did not force children to sit all day quietly. Instead, they were encouraged to run and play. And the adults were not required to spend the day seated on hard benches, in contemplative prayer. Also, no one in the Miller family wore their heavy, black Sunday clothing on visiting Sundays. Everyone simply wore comfortable, clean clothes. Instead of donning her black church dress, Eve had put on the brand-new peach-colored dress Rosemary had made for her.

The other difference Eve noticed that morning, her first Visiting Sunday with Levi's family, was how kind and gentle everyone was to each other in the house. It was as if on this day, they set aside the business of their lives to be sure they were living the lives God meant for them. There were no disagreements at the breakfast table, no chastising, only kind words exchanged and gentle laughter.

"Chloe!" Tara called, her arm linked through Eve's as they approached three picnic tables where the women were gathered.

As in Lancaster County, the married women naturally sat together, and the unmarried gathered separately. Without hearing a word said, Eve knew that the married women talked of children and housekeeping, while the younger women chattered about boys, singings and their dreams of the men they would marry. Eve didn't feel like she belonged with either group so she was happy to go along with whatever Tara wanted.

"Chloe!" Tara called. "Here she is. Eve."

Several married women looked in their direction, and Eve felt herself blush. Rosemary had introduced her to them all earlier, before Eve found an excuse to escape to the kitchen, but as with Levi's family, it was all so overwhelming. Everyone knew who she was, knew her name and where she'd come from, but they were all mixed up in her head now. Chloe, however, she had not met because Eve had fled to the security of the kitchen before she and her family arrived.

Tara and Eve stopped short as a little girl in a pink dress and adorable white apron toddled in front of them on unsteady legs. Hot on her heels was Ginger's little girl, Lizzy, who was four.

"Come back, Ada!" Lizzy cried. Then she called over her shoulder to one of the mothers, "I'll get her!"

Tara's friend Chloe walked across the freshly cut grass to meet them. Chloe's hair, covered mostly by her prayer *kapp*, was so blond that it looked white. And when the young woman grew nearer, Eve saw that her eyebrows and lashes were the same hue.

"It's *goot* to meet you, Eve," Chloe said. "Nice to meet someone else new to Hickory Grove. We only moved here a few weeks ago."

"Tara! Tara, come here! I want to meet Levi's wife."

Eve turned at the same time as Chloe and Tara to see a woman in her forties waving them to where she sat in a lawn chair. Ada's mother, also a new arrival. "I want to meet Eve."

Tara leaned over and whispered in Eve's ear, "Sorry."

"For what?" Eve whispered back.

Tara only opened her eyes wider in a *you'll see soon enough* expression. Then, side by side, the three young women approached the older woman beckoning them.

"This is Eunice Gruber," Tara introduced. "They live down the road. I think you met her son John at church last week. Cute with the fuzzy eyebrows," she added in a whisper in Eve's ear.

Eve forced a smile and nodded to Eunice. "Glad to meet you."

Eunice was a slender woman with broad cheeks and a birthmark on her chin. "I was surprised to hear Levi had married so suddenly," the older woman said, coming to her feet.

That didn't take long, Eve thought.

"When the family came home from church—I missed it, because little Ada was running a fever— and my husband told me Levi had brought a bride home from Lancaster County, I said Barnabas, you don't know what you're talking about." She shooed away a fly buzzing around her head. "I said, I'd know if Levi had married." She opened her thin arms wide. "And now, come to find out, I was wrong."

Not sure what to say, Eve just stood there between Chloe and Tara.

As it turned out, she didn't have to say anything because Eunice kept talking. "I thought for certain Rosemary would have told me Levi was marrying, us being such good friends." She narrowed her gaze. "But then I started to wonder. What if Rosemary and Benjamin *didn't know* Levi was marrying? What if they had eloped?" She leaned closer. "Did you elope?"

Eve froze in panic, unsure how to respond.

Eunice took another step toward Eve. "Well, did you? What town are you from in Lancaster County? Maybe I know your family."

Eve felt her heart thud in her chest. She didn't know what to say.

"*Ach!* Here come the men," Tara cried, looking in the direction of the barns. "And I don't even have the ice cream out." She grabbed Eve's arm. "Would you help me, Eve, else I know my *mam* will be cross with me." She began to pull Eve in the direction of the house, calling over her shoulder, "Talk to you later, Eunice!"

"Wait! I'm coming, too," Chloe declared, hurrying across the grass.

Eve heaved a sigh of relief and linked her arm through Tara's, thankful her new friend had rescued her from what was bound to have become a more uncomfortable situation than it already was.

"If you haven't already figured it out," Tara explained as the young women made a beeline for the house, "you've just met Hickory Grove's gossip. Eunice knows everything, and what she doesn't know, *she finds out*."

Chloe giggled. "We had a Eunice back in Washington State. Her name was Trudy. She was always repeating other people's business."

Eve looked from Tara on one side of her to Chloe on the other.

"Did she tell the truth?" Tara asked. "Because Eunice isn't just nosy. She doesn't always get the facts right. When my *mam* had her surgery on her foot last year, she told Mary Fisher's mother that *Mam* was in the family way again. Then Eunice had gone on about how *Mam* was too old for babies, that James and Josiah were proof of that, and that she ought to be ashamed of herself."

"Ne!" Chloe exclaimed, her eyes growing round. "She did not!"

"Ya, and my twin brothers just learning to walk!" Tara led Eve and Chloe up the steps to the porch. "See, I told you you would like Chloe," she told Eve. "I know Chloe and I aren't married, but I still think we can be the best of friends, don't you?"

So relieved that Tara had saved her from Eunice's questioning, Eve almost threw her arms around Levi's sister. *"Ya*, I think we can be." She put her hands together the way she had already seen Rosemary do several times. "Now let's get that ice cream to our guests."

A short time later, the three young women were set up at one of the picnic tables. There, they scooped the last of the three gallons of homemade strawberry ice cream out of the plastic containers. Almost at the bottom of her tub, Eve looked up to see the last person in her line to get the homemade treat. She gulped.

It was Levi.

She'd been so busy with the task that she hadn't even seen him. "One scoop or two?" she asked, pushing the heavy spoon down into the tub.

"Three if you've got it. Tara makes the best strawberry ice cream I've ever had." He handed her a bowl.

"There's enough," she said softly, keeping her eyes down.

"And enough for you, too? If there isn't, we can split it."

Eve considered telling him she wasn't going to have ice cream. Back home, her father had often criticized her taste for sweets. But then, glancing around, she noticed that the young folks, married and unmarried, were settling down as couples to have their dessert. Even Ginger and her husband, who had four children by his previous marriage, were stealing a few minutes of time alone together.

This is what we need, Eve thought. *Levi and I need to spend time together to get to know each other.* And then, before she lost her nerve, she said, "*Ya*, Husband, there's enough for me, too. I thought we could have ours together. Under that tree," she dared, indicating an oak tree with her ice cream scoop.

Levi hesitated, chewing on the idea for a moment, then murmured, "*Ya*, I think that would be nice. Wife," he added.

Chapter Five

Eve's shy smile softened Levi's heart. And he was reminded that it didn't take much to make her happy—
just a smile, a kind word, an extra moment of his time.

All week he'd been tense, annoyed with everything
and everyone. And that had included his wife. But the
way she looked at him now made him want to be a better man, a better husband. As he studied her rosy cheeks
and pretty mouth, he thought of what Jacob had said
the other day about being patient with Eve. His brother
was right. Change had come quickly to her life as well
as his, and she deserved patience from him.

As much as Levi hated to admit it, his little brother
was probably right about their father, too. By returning home six months early, Levi had changed the time-
line for expanding the buggy shop. With him home
now, their father had been forced to build before he
was ready, but also put out money he hadn't planned
on spending yet. New construction was never cheap,
and the up-front cost of purchasing the materials they

needed to build a good, sturdy buggy wasn't inexpensive, either.

"There you go. The last drop," Eve said, pouring the last bit of melted ice cream into Levi's bowl.

Levi blinked, bringing himself back to the moment. "Here, let me take yours, too." He picked up both bowls.

"I'll get our spoons. And napkins." She grabbed the utensils and moved a rock they were using to hold down the napkins, so they didn't blow away. "Oh, dear. There's only one left." She held up the paper napkin.

He shrugged. "We'll share. Come on. Let's go sit down and dig into this before it all melts."

"Are you sure?" she fretted, following him. "I could go up to the house and get more napkins."

He stopped, reminding himself that her legs were much shorter than his, and he waited for her to catch up. "I'm not letting this ice cream melt. By the time you got back from the house, we'd be drinking it." He smiled at her, feeling like his old self. "We'll share the napkin, and if I'm too messy, I'll just use my shirt." He demonstrated by rolling his shoulder forward and wiping his mouth on his shirtsleeve.

She giggled and the sound made his heart sing. He hadn't known Eve very long, and he didn't know her well, but he liked making her happy. Something about the way she smiled at him brought a tightness to his chest. The good kind.

"Here?" he asked, gesturing with her smaller bowl of ice cream at the tree she'd picked out.

"Ya." She sat down in the soft green grass, and he handed her the bowl before sitting beside her.

His back against the tree trunk, Levi accepted the

spoon she offered and dipped it into his bowl. The ice cream was smooth and cold and sweet on his tongue. "Mmm. Delicious. Tara has always made a good straw-berry ice cream, but I think this is the best she's ever made." He cut his eyes at her. "Did you help her make this?"

Eve licked her spoon, nodded. "*Ya.* I showed her how to sugar the strawberries and let them sit before you mash them." She pointed her spoon at him. "But the real trick is to add a little bit of fresh lemon juice to the strawberries to brighten their flavor. Mind you, not to the milk," she warned. "It could curdle."

He laughed. "Good to know, but I hate to tell you, Eve, I'm not going to be making ice cream. If we have ice cream in our house, it's going to be ice cream you've made or something I bought at Byler's store."

She smiled and dug into her bowl. "Ice cream is so good on a warm day like this. Sweet, but not too sweet," she told him.

He watched her, enjoying the pleasure he saw on her face as she sampled the cold confection. "Oops, you've got a little—" He picked up the napkin she'd tucked be-tween them and blotted her chin.

She looked up at him through her lashes, seeming embarrassed and pleased at the same time. "Got it?" she asked.

Levi was surprised to find how much he enjoyed such an intimate moment between them. A moment he didn't want to end.

"Levi?"

"Got it." He pulled his hand away and tucked the

napkin into his pocket. "I like the dress, Eve. It's a good color on you."

She ran her hand down the skirt of her new hunter-green dress. "Rosemary made it for me. She was going to make me a blue one—blue's my favorite color for a dress—but she didn't have any blue fabric." Seeming to have second thoughts, she looked up at him. "Not that I'm not grateful that she made this for me. It's been a very long time since I had a new dress and I love it."

Levi leaned his head against the trunk of the tree. It felt good to just sit here with Eve, to relax and enjoy the Sunday afternoon. The air smelled of early summer: freshly cut grass, sunshine and honeysuckle. Around him, he could hear the muffled chatter of his family and their friends, and in the distance, the bleat of one of his brother's goats and the lowing of their cows. "Tell me why blue dresses are your favorite, Eve."

She glanced away, giving him a moment to study her. She had a round face with rosy cheeks and long, dark lashes that framed her brown eyes. She had gorgeous eyes; he didn't know how he hadn't noticed that before. The color of hot chocolate, they were big and round and expressive.

"My *mam* always wore blue. It makes me think of her. I had a blue dress before, but—" She shook her head. "It doesn't matter now," she mumbled.

He took another bite of ice cream that was bursting with bits of fresh strawberry. "When did your mother die?"

"Twelve years ago." She lowered her gaze to the ice cream on her lap, her voice soft. "Childbirth. The baby didn't make it, either."

His first impulse was to reach out and touch her to comfort her, but that didn't seem right. Married or not, they were still strangers. And what if she didn't want him to touch her? He spoke instead, hoping his words would be of some comfort. "I'm so sorry, Eve. I have an idea what that's like. I lost my *mam* six years ago. Cancer. I wasn't young like you were. I was already in my twenties, but—" He shrugged.

Instead of looking away, Eve met his gaze. "It's hard to lose a mother. It doesn't matter how old you are." She smiled sadly as if recalling a good memory. "I still miss my *mam* every day."

"Me, too," he agreed, tapping his spoon on the rim of his bowl. "My *mam* was a good mother, a good woman and always full of fun. She used to play practical jokes on my father all the time. One time, she packed him a lunch and put a note inside his sandwich." He smiled at the memory, surprised by the emotion it evoked. He couldn't have been more than nine or ten when it happened. "My *dat* took a big bite right out of the paper before he realized it was there."

Her eyes grew even rounder. "Was he upset with her?"

Levi looked at her, drawing back. "My *dat*?" He chuckled. "He thought it was hilarious, even though his friends teased him about it for years."

She smiled and then asked, "Was it... Did it feel strange when your father married again?"

Scooping a last spoonful of ice cream, he considered his reply. "Yes and no," he said slowly. "I knew Rosemary and her husband, Ethan, before my *mam* died. *Dat* and Ethan were best friends, so he was always around.

Rosemary, too, and the girls. Jesse. Rosemary helped care for my *mam* in the end."

Levi licked the back of his spoon, disappointed his ice cream was gone. It really was the best strawberry ice cream he'd ever had, and he was proud that his wife had made it. She was a good cook, that was already obvious, and that had been one of the traits he'd wanted in a wife.

People assumed that all Amish women were good cooks, but that wasn't true. His sister Mary, who still lived in Upstate New York with her husband and children, was an awful cook. It was a family joke. Levi still remembered their mother teasing Mary on her wedding day, saying her husband, Jake, must have been madly in love with her to marry her, knowing she would never learn to make a decent *hasenpfeffer*.

"Was that hard?" Eve pressed, her brown eyes on him. "Having a new mother?"

"Well, I was old enough that she didn't become a mother to me. Not in the way my *mam* had been, at least. When it happened, it felt…right." He looked up to find her listening intently. She hadn't asked the question just to make conversation; she really wanted to know.

"My father was devastated after my mother died," he continued. "And it was the same for Rosemary." He shrugged. "It seemed natural that they should come together in their grieving, and when it became something more…" He exhaled. "It seemed God's will to me. To all of us." He hesitated when he saw a sadness come over her. "I know it wasn't the same for you when your father remarried. I'm sorry for that."

Her bowl empty, she took his and stacked them together in the grass. "My stepmother was nothing like Rosemary."

He chuckled. "No one is like our Rosemary. Before she and *Dat* wed, she came to each of my brothers and me, and to my sister, and told us she would never try to take the place of our mother. But she hoped, she said, that she could be something between a second mother and a friend to us. And she's been that. And more importantly, she's been a good wife to my father. She makes him happy."

When Levi glanced at his wife, he saw that she was smiling at him. "They have a happy marriage," he went on. "The kind of marriage I hope that one day you and I will have, Eve." This time, before he could think better of it, he covered her small hand with his.

She looked up at him. "I want that, too, Levi. For us to be a happy couple." She looked away and then back at him again. "But how can that be if we never see each other?"

Levi felt the prickly heat of defensiveness on the back of his neck. "We see each other."

"Not enough," she answered. "You work such long hours. I only see you for meals. I want to spend more time like this with you."

She smiled up at him, but he didn't smile back. Suddenly he was feeling the weight of his father's disappointment on his shoulders again. His father wasn't happy with him, and now his wife was telling him that she wasn't, either?

Levi pulled his hand away. "I work hard all day, Eve. To earn our keep here. And to make a life for us." He pointed in the direction of the barn. "Jacob and I broke our backs this week, putting those walls up to expand the buggy shop. I did that for us. For you."

"Levi, I didn't mean—"

He interrupted her without allowing her to continue. "Do you not understand that the buggies I build in that new workshop space will give us the means to have a house, to put food on our table? I assume that's what you want? A house of your own? Or do you want to live under my father's roof for the rest of our lives?"

She folded her hands in her lap, averting her gaze. "I wasn't criticizing you, Levi."

He stood up. Everyone else was finishing up their ice cream, too. The couples were parting, and the men were gathering to head back to the barn to see the airbags he was going to install in the buggy he would be building. As he turned back to his wife, he spotted Rosemary watching them.

"Stand up," he told Eve without looking at her.

"What?"

"Please stand up." He put out his hand to help her. "And smile."

She came to her feet and moved in front of him, forcing him to look at her. "Levi, please. I didn't mean to—"

"Smile," he repeated. "People are watching us. It wouldn't do to see us arguing. We're supposed to be the happy newlyweds."

"I wasn't arguing with you, Levi. I only—"

He held his exaggerated smile, frozen on his face. She went silent and forced a smile.

"*Danke.* Now, I'm going back down to the barn. I'll

see you at supper." As Levi walked away, he could feel Eve's gaze on his back.

And once again, he felt her discontent with him.

Eve turned the wooden handle on the glass butter churn as hard as she could, watching specks of yellow appear in the thick, rich cream. It was a rainy afternoon, and the women of the household were all gathered in the kitchen. Rosemary was pressing the wrinkles out of a prayer *kapp* from a whole pile of clean *kapps*, while Tara was making sourdough bread. Nettie's sleeves were rolled up as she scoured the gas stovetop vigorously. And Ginger had come to visit, bringing her two youngest, and was busy shucking early peas she'd brought from her garden.

"I was talking to Chloe yesterday," Tara announced as she turned dough from a bowl onto the kitchen table across from where Eve sat, churning the butter. "She came with her aunt to the greenhouse to buy flowers, and Chloe said that her aunt said that we might be splitting up our church district." She became more distressed with each word. "Chloe asked me what I knew about it, and I told her not a thing. Is that true, *Mam*? Are we splitting up our church?"

"Tara, you and I have talked about gossiping," Rosemary admonished with a sigh. "Let no unwholesome talk come out of your mouth, but only what helps others."

Tara raised her floured hands. "But it's not gossip if it's true. Is it true? I don't want to split our church. We've been going to church with the same folks since we came to Hickory Grove."

"Calm yourself, dear." Rosemary picked up a can of spray starch and shook it. Something rattled inside.

Eve was fascinated by the canned starch. Back home, she had mixed powdered starch in warm water, dipped her and her sisters' *kapps* in it, let it dry and then pressed it. The way Rosemary was doing it wasn't nearly so messy and made much more sense, especially with a whole house full of women.

"Wait." Nettie turned from the stove, steel wool in her hand. She was wearing pink rubber gloves so she wouldn't burn her hands with the caustic cleaner she was using. "Are we changing churches? Does that mean we won't go with the Fishers anymore?"

"Nettie's sweet on Jeb Fisher," Tara explained to Eve.

"She's doing it again, *Mam*," Nettie said. "Make her stop."

Rosemary sighed. "Doing what, dear?"

"Teasing me about Jeb. I keep telling her we're just friends."

"Maybe." Tara giggled. "But she'd like them to be more. That's why she doesn't want our church to split up." She turned her attention to Eve again. "Because then she couldn't sit in the women's pews and stare across the aisle at Jeb every other Sunday."

Eve turned the crank of the churn harder as she followed the conversation. The butter was forming into chunks now. She loved the process, feeling the soft, squishy butter in her hands, adding just the right amount of salt and waiting to see if the blocks came out of the wooden mold in perfect shapes.

Nettie walked to the sink and tossed the pad of steel wool in. "Is there any truth to what she's saying, *Mam*?"

She rinsed a clean washrag and walked back to the stove to wipe it off. "Why would our church split?"

Rosemary gave the *kapp* a good spray of starch. "For the same reason our church split back in New York. Too many people. With so many Amish moving to Hickory Grove, the church districts are getting too big. We have to be able to fit everyone under one roof for services, and with Chloe's family just arrived, we now have thirteen families. It's becoming unmanageable."

"But wouldn't the new families just start their own church?" Nettie asked.

Rosemary lifted the iron off the woodstove and when she skimmed it over the white *kapp*, it sizzled. "I don't know how it will be done, if it will be done, but my guess is that established families will have the opportunity to become a part of a new district, mixing the old with the new." She tilted her head one way and then the other. "Some families will go, some will stay."

"They did just that in Seven Hickories. I bumped into Hannah Hartman in Byler's store the other day, and she said that she and Albert and her daughter Susanna and her husband all joined the new church district." Ginger glanced Eve's way. "Hannah's second husband is Albert Hartman. He used to be Mennonite, and he's our vet. When they married, he became Amish, and the bishop lets him drive a truck for work."

An Amish man with a truck? Eve couldn't imagine.

"Well, I don't know if I get a say," Nettie went on, as she wiped the stove down. "But if I do, I want to stay. I like our district."

"Nothing has been decided, *Dochter*. It hasn't even

been decided that we'll be forming a new district. We're just talking."

"See, then I wasn't gossiping," Tara declared happily. "I was passing on information that Nettie didn't know."

Eve unscrewed the lid on the glass churn and dumped the ball of butter into a clean cloth.

As she began to squeeze the liquid out of the yellow butter, the back door opened, and she heard the scrape of heavy boots. She recognized the rhythm of her husband's footsteps and a moment later Levi walked into the kitchen with Ginger and Eli's son Philip in his arms. The five-year-old was holding a clean rag to his nose, and it was clear he'd been crying.

"*Ach*, what happened?" Ginger set the pan of peas on the table and walked over.

As she made her way across the kitchen, Eve caught a glimpse of a slightly rounded belly beneath her apron and dress. She was obviously in the family way. Eve didn't know how she had missed it. No one had mentioned that Ginger and Eli were expecting, but that wasn't all that unusual. Of course women talked among themselves in quilting circles, but pregnancy wasn't something normally discussed in the presence of Amish men, even if the men were brothers or stepfathers.

Levi lowered the boy to the floor. "Just a little bloody nose. He was chasing one of the cats through the buggy shop, tripped and—" He shrugged. "It happens."

Ginger lifted her skirt and knelt in front of Phillip. "Let me see."

"I'm fine," Phillip said, his voice muffled by the cloth.

Ginger peeled away the rag and studied the red spots. "Tilt your head back."

The boy did as he was told.

"Looks like it's stopped bleeding," Ginger declared.

Phillip tried to pull away from his mother. "Can I go back out and play?"

The boy looked just like his father, Eli. Eve had learned from Tara, not Levi, that Eli's wife had passed a few years ago and that Ginger had been watching Eli's children for him while he worked. Their relationship had blossomed from friendship to love, and Ginger had married Eli, getting a ready-made family in the bargain, only a few months ago. Ginger was good with the children, and they adored her, so much so that Eve would never have guessed they'd been born to a different mother.

"Please, Ginger?" Phillip begged. "Can I go back to the barn with Levi?"

"I think you best stay inside in case it starts bleeding again." Ginger got to her feet and dropped the bloody rag into the trash can. "Go find Lizzy and Josiah and James. I think they're playing on the upstairs landing."

Phillip groaned, flopping his hands to his sides. "I don't want to play with babies."

"Your sister is hardly a baby." Ginger looked in Eve's direction. "At home, Lizzy may be the youngest, but she runs things. She's put herself in charge of her brothers, all three of them. And mostly they do as they're told." She looked to Levi. "Thank you for bringing him up to the house. I'm sorry if he was any trouble."

"No trouble at all. I just thought I best bring him in."

Levi turned to go, making no point to acknowledge

Eve in the room. She tried not to be hurt. Men came and went all day, she told herself. If they stopped to say hello and goodbye every time, no one would ever get anything done.

"Oh, Levi," Ginger called after him. "Did Jesse give you the message about your dental appointment?"

He turned back, frowning. "I didn't get a message."

She rolled her eyes. "I stopped at the harness shop on the way up the lane this morning. Trudy was busy ringing up a customer, so I answered the phone. Your dentist's office called to say they had a cancellation Friday. They can fix your broken filling at two thirty."

"I saw Jesse. He didn't say anything."

Ginger rolled her eyes. "Boys. Anyway, I said you would take the appointment." She grimaced. "I hope that's all right."

"Friday? That's good, isn't it?" Rosemary remarked, returning the iron to the top of the woodstove, taking care to grasp it by the wooden handle so as not to burn herself. "I'm surprised you got in so quickly. You should go with him, Eve."

When Eve looked up, Rosemary was looking right at her. She glanced at Levi, not sure what to say. She would love to go to Dover with him, but he didn't seem so keen on the idea from the look on his face.

Levi shuffled his feet. "I… I don't know that Eve wants to ride all the way into Dover and back, just to sit in a waiting room."

"Nonsense, Levi. Your wife would enjoy getting out of the house and spending time with you." She turned to Eve. "Wouldn't you, *Dochter*?"

Eve loved that Rosemary had begun referring to her

as her daughter. She had no one else to call her that, and it made her feel good. Like a part of Levi's family. "*Ya*, that would be nice," she managed. "I haven't been to town yet."

Levi opened his mouth, closed it and then opened it again. "Rosemary—"

"Then this will be a perfect chance," Rosemary said, talking over Levi. "And on the way home, you can stop at Spence's Bazaar and get me some thread from the fabric shop we like. I'll show you what color I need." She directed this toward Eve. "Levi would never find it on his own."

"We can do that for you." Eve made eye contact with Levi. He didn't look pleased, but he didn't look angry, either. Just…resigned.

"Anyone else have anything for Eve and me to do?" he asked, a hint of sarcasm in his voice. "*Ne?* Then I best get back to work."

Eve watched her husband put his straw hat back on his head and walk out the door. Then she returned to squeezing the freshly made butter dry, excited at the prospect of an afternoon out with her husband.

Chapter Six

Levi walked down the dentist's office hallway, his straw hat in his hand, looking for the exit sign. The place was a warren of hallways and doors. As he looked for a sign pointing him in the right direction, he massaged his jaw that felt like pins and needles the way his foot did when it went to sleep. His beard stubble still felt odd to him. As odd as the idea that he was a married man.

Seeing an exit sign at last, he walked to the door—only to realize it was an emergency exit. He backtracked. Eve was sitting patiently in the waiting room. He couldn't believe that Rosemary had invited Eve to go with him to his appointment. If he didn't like Rosemary so much, he might have told her so. It wasn't that he didn't want Eve to come with him, only that he wanted to make that choice for himself. He wanted to invite his wife on an outing himself.

Of course, he probably wouldn't have thought to bring Eve along if Rosemary hadn't suggested it in front of everyone the other day. That night in their bedroom, he had been cranky about the idea of Eve going, but she'd been so excited when he'd pulled the buggy up in front of the house that he felt guilty for not having thought to invite her himself. And Eve hadn't wanted to go just because she wanted to see Dover. She had come because she wanted to be with him. That was what she had told him on the buggy ride.

"Looking for the exit?" a woman in pink scrubs asked as she walked by him in the hall.

"Yes. I thought it was this way, but it wasn't."

"Don't sweat it," she said. "I've worked here for almost a year, and I still get confused sometimes." She laughed, pointing in the opposite direction. "Take a right down the next hallway, then the second door on your left. It's marked."

"Thank you," he told her with a nod.

"No problem!" she sang.

Levi followed her directions and was relieved to find Eve waiting in a chair. She rose when she saw him.

"Are you okay?" she asked him in Pennsylvania Deitsch. "You were in there a long time."

"Ya, oll recht." He switched to English because his father had taught him to speak the language that prevailed in a room. He said it made people uncomfortable when others around them were speaking a language they didn't know. So Levi spoke Deitsch among the Amish, and when with Englishers, he spoke English. "I'm still numb, but it didn't hurt." He glanced across the waiting room to a TV mounted on the wall. A commercial for bed mattresses blasted. He pointed at it. "Were you watching?"

"Ya. I was. That's not a problem, is it?"

He went to the door that opened into the parking lot and she followed. She was an interesting woman, especially considering the home she had come from. He had met Amon Summy only twice, but that was enough times to know that the man was a controlling bully. Having lived under his roof, Eve would have been meeker, more docile, he thought. She was pleasantly surprising him. She spoke her mind in such an innocent way, like when she had told him the Sunday before that they weren't spending enough time together. Levi had taken it as criticism then, but with a little distance from the moment, he realized she was only telling him how she was feeling. And as her husband, he knew he needed to learn to listen.

"What were you watching?" he asked curiously. They stood for a moment in the lobby, looking out the glass doors. It was raining.

"A cooking show. How to make a buckle. Any kind. You start with the same basic recipe and then change up the fruit."

"What's the difference between a fruit buckle and a cobbler?" he asked.

"That's easy." She looked up at him through her long, thick lashes. "A cobbler has fruit on the bottom and biscuit on top. With a buckle, it's cake and fruit mixed together, with a crunchy streusel on top."

She looked nice today in the new green dress Rosemary had made for her, a fresh white apron and a starched *kapp* over her dark hair. Her cheeks were rosy and her dark eyes sparkled. It was funny that the first time he had ever met Eve, before the day in the barn that had sealed both their fates, he hadn't thought she was particularly pretty. But beginning the day they had stood before the bishop and exchanged vows, he had started to see her differently. Now, there were times when he looked at her and felt she *was* pretty.

"I like buckles and cobblers." He held up one finger. "And crisps, too. I love an apple crisp made from a mix of apples."

She nodded enthusiastically. "Me, too. I put cinnamon and vanilla in the oatmeal crumble that goes on top of my apple crisp."

Levi rubbed his stomach. "Just talking about it makes me hungry." He glanced out the glass door. "Looks like the rain's let up a bit. We should go. You want me to bring the buggy around for you so you don't get wet?"

She laughed. "I won't melt if you don't."

He smiled and reached for the door.

"Levi?"

He let go and the glass door swung closed. *"Ya?"*

She folded her hands in front of her. "Do you not want me to watch TV when I'm in a waiting room?"

He knitted his brow. "What?"

"The TV. I'm asking you—" she looked down at her black sneakers that had a hole in the toe "—because if you don't want me to see TV, I... I'll sit with my back to it next time."

"You're asking me if you can watch a cooking show in a doctor's waiting room?"

She nibbled on her lower lip. "Well...you being the man of the house, you have the final say in—" She exhaled. "In everything. If you tell me not to watch TV, I won't." She paused again. "Though I have to say, I don't think there's any harm in it once in a while. I mean, to see a cooking show."

"Eve, I would hope that I would never *tell* you to do or not do anything. I may be the man of our house—even if we don't have a house yet—but I hope that we'll be able to discuss matters. I want your opinion on things, and I hope you want mine."

She stared at him for a long moment, then said, "I knew you were a good man when I married you. Because you asked me to marry you when you heard what had happened, but—" She glanced away, then back at him. "But Levi, you're even a better man than I thought."

He just stood there for a moment, not sure what to say. He was touched that she felt that way and was willing to tell him. He tried to be a good man, but he knew he failed in small ways every single day. Her confidence in him made him want to try even harder. Except he wasn't sure how to go about that. A man was supposed to court a woman before they married. They should have spent weeks, even months, going to singings together, having supper with each other's families, taking buggy rides together on visiting Sundays. When he had impulsively offered to marry Eve, none of that had crossed his mind.

When he looked down, he found Eve watching him—waiting for him to say something.

Levi cleared his throat. "I think there's no harm in learning how to make a good buckle for your husband, even if it is from a TV in a waiting room," he told her, lightening the tone of the conversation. "Especially if it's a blueberry buckle. That's my favorite." He glanced out the glass door again. "Now, if we're going to get that thread for Rosemary, we better go before the sky opens up again."

Then he held the door open for his wife the way he had seen Englishers do.

Levi checked his pocket watch, a gift from his father when he started his first job at fifteen years old. It was three thirty. Jacob had gone into the hardware store to get a primer for the walls of the buggy shop, as well as another box of nails, leaving Levi to finish mudding the drywall. He should have been back by now. He should have been back forty-five minutes ago.

He dipped his blade into a tray of mud and dragged it over a seam in the drywall. If it had been up to him, he wouldn't have put up the shop's drywall—bare studs would have suited him fine—but their father had insisted the walls be finished. He said he took pride in his workspace, and Levi needed to do the same.

Levi scraped away the excess mud and moved on to the next tape-covered seam. It wasn't that he didn't take pride in the place where he worked; it was only that he was in a hurry to get started. Working alone, it would take him a full month to build a buggy. And now, with most of the supplies having arrived, he was eager to get to work.

His father walked in through the open bay door, carrying two boxes. "Another UPS delivery," he announced.

Levi glanced over his shoulder. Things between him and his father had been awkward since his return to Hickory Grove. His *dat* had not once brought up the circumstances of his hasty marriage, but he didn't have to. Levi knew what he was thinking. He could see the disappointment in his father's eyes every time he looked at him.

"Should be the mechanism for the airbags. Folks can adjust them according to how big a load they're carrying," Levi explained. It was considered new technology, and it might cause a stir in some of the church districts in the county, but he liked the idea of bringing progress to his community in a good way. He also had plans for better headlamps and taillights, which ran off a simple battery. The brighter LED lights would make a buggy easier to see in the dark and, therefore, safer.

Levi watched his father set down the boxes without responding. He'd missed talking with his father when he was away and had been looking forward to the conversations they would have again when he returned. He'd been home three weeks now, and his father was still ignoring him for the most part. His *dat* answered him when spoken to, but he didn't initiate any conversation, and Levi was beginning to feel as if he were the naughty child put in a corner as punishment. And he was becoming more frustrated by the day because this behavior was so unlike his father. When he'd first arrived, he had assumed his *dat* would get past his displeasure and their relationship would return to what it had been, but now he feared that would never happen. Several times in the last week, Levi had almost said something to his *dat*, then bit his tongue.

But suddenly he couldn't hold back any longer. *"Dat,"* he said, setting his putty knife down.

His father was restocking the boxes, his back to him.

"Dat," Levi repeated a little louder.

His father turned to him. *"Ya?"*

"Dat, I'm sorry that I've disappointed you, but…" He exhaled and glanced away, beginning to wish he had kept his mouth shut. But it was too late now. "I know that this is not how you wanted to see me married," he went on, choosing his words carefully. "But what's done is done. I'm tired of being treated like a schoolboy who's misbehaved. I'm beginning to feel like you don't want me here. Want us," he added. "I'm starting to worry that maybe Eve and I should have stayed in Lancaster."

His father slid his hands into his denim pockets, looking down at the floor. He, too, was choosing his words carefully. "I've been wondering… Have you talked with the bishop?"

Levi's brow furrowed. "I saw him Sunday. We chatted during the meal."

"I mean…" His father cleared his throat. "Have you talked to him about you and Eve?"

Levi stared at his father for a moment, still not following. Then it hit him. What he was asking was if Levi had gone to the bishop and confessed his sin of relations before marriage. "I have not because there's no need," he answered stiffly.

The older man, the man Levi had looked up to his entire life, took his time in responding. He seemed to be turning Levi's words over in his head. At last he said, "You know that I love you."

Levi's eyes suddenly felt scratchy. "I do."

"I'm sorry if I've made you think I didn't want you here because that's not true." His father slowly lifted his gaze. "But I never expected this from you, out of all of your brothers. And to think that a son of mine would not confess to his sin…" He paused, then cleared his throat and went on. "As I told you the day you arrived, I still need some time, *Sohn*."

"How much time?" Levi asked, wishing desperately that he could tell his father that he hadn't sinned, so no confession was necessary.

Benjamin shook his head. "I can't answer that right now. Rosemary is saying the same, and I can't give her an answer, either. Both of you—all of you—will just have to be patient with me."

"All of us? Who else has talked to you about this?" Levi asked.

"Tara." The barest smile appeared on his lips. "She accused me of being mean. She likes Eve. We all do. I'm not trying to be mean. I just need time to work through this."

His father went silent, and for a long moment, Levi just stood there. He hadn't thought seriously about going back to Lancaster, but he wondered if maybe that would be best for him the way he was feeling today.

He reached for the spackling compound blade again and scooped up some mud to continue his drywall work. "Where is Jacob with those nails?" he muttered.

Eve took the croquet mallet Jacob handed her and stared at the blue wooden ball resting in the grass in front of her. She looked up at him apprehensively. "I just hit it?"

"Just hit it through the wire thingies!" Tara called from twenty feet away. She had already taken her turn and had managed to hit her red ball all the way to the foot of a poplar tree that was outside the playing area. Jacob had instructed her to move it back inside and forfeit a turn.

Jacob looked to Eve. "Don't listen to her. They're called wickets. Just hit the ball with the mallet, so it will roll through these first two wickets." He pointed at the two wire arches directly in front of the wooden stake in the ground, which was the starting point.

Eve held her breath and then tapped the blue ball ever so gently. It rolled halfway under the first wicket and stopped in a tuft of grass. She groaned. "I can't do this. I'm terrible at games."

"*Ya*, you can," Tara insisted, running toward them.

While she looked for more jelly jars in the cellar that morning, Tara had discovered the croquet set, practically new in a bag, left by the previous owners. After cleaning up from the midday meal, she had insisted Eve help her set up the game in the front yard. The fact that Eve had never played croquet, had never even seen the game, didn't matter to Tara. And in the end, Eve had agreed to help because she couldn't say no to Tara. Her new friend had been so kind and generous since her arrival. Tara made a point every day to include Eve not just in the work of the day, but in the family, as well as any fun that was to be had. And if there was one thing Tara knew, it was how to have fun. She reminded Eve so much of her sister Annie that it hurt sometimes.

Tara and Eve had been following the written instructions in the bag to set up the playing field when Jacob returned from town. He'd fetched some lime from the barn and marked the field with the white powder, then helped them place the remainder of the wickets at the correct distance.

"You have to hit it harder than that," Tara told Eve as she came to a sliding halt, bumping into her and Jacob.

Jacob caught his stepsister by the arm and ducked to keep from being hit by the wooden mallet in her hand. "Easy," he warned good-naturedly.

Eve turned sideways, caught her lower lip between her teeth and hit her ball. Except that this time she hit it too hard and at a bad angle. It flew through the grass, hit the brick edging of a flower bed filled with orange daylilies and popped into the bed. A disgruntled toad hopped out of the flower bed.

Tara burst into laughter, and Eve and Jacob laughed with her.

"Okay, that might be a little too hard," Jacob told her. He leaned down and placed his green ball at the starting point. "I'll go get your ball. You hit this one. Hit it harder than the first time, not as hard as the second."

"*Ne*, I'll get it!" Tara took off, swinging her mallet in her hand like a windmill.

"Okay, okay." Eve nodded again and again, telling herself she could do this. The game seemed like it would be so much fun, especially on a warm, breezy day like today. She hadn't played games outside since she was eleven or twelve, though she had loved them as a child. Her father saw no need for a girl that old to play anymore. He thought his daughters' places were inside the house, cooking and cleaning, or in the garden weeding. Anytime he saw one of his children idle, he found them another chore to do.

Eve pulled back the mallet, concentrating so hard

on lining up behind the green ball that she swung back too far and hit her ankle. "Ouch!" she cried, laughing as she dropped the mallet.

"It's not supposed to be a dangerous game," Levi's brother told her, trying not to laugh as she jumped up and down in pain. He picked up her mallet. "You okay?"

"She's fine!" Tara hollered back as she dug Eve's ball out of the flower bed. "Try again," she told Eve. "It took me forever to learn how to play, and now I love it. We play it at the Fishers' all the time."

Eve looked up at Jacob. Like Tara, he'd gone out of his way to welcome her into their family. But while Tara seemed oblivious, she had an idea that Jacob suspected something wasn't right between Eve and Levi. He'd just been polite enough, so far, not to bring it up. "I'm fine," she told him, reaching for the mallet. "I just don't know how to hold this thing." She turned sideways again, eyeing the green ball.

Jacob stepped behind her and reached out to turn the mallet slightly in her hands. "You have to hit the ball squarely. It's all about hitting it square on, every time," he explained. "That'll keep it out of Rosemary's flower beds and all of us out of trouble."

She laughed. "Like this?" She adjusted the mallet in her hand.

"Almost." He reached from behind her and turned it slightly.

She stared at the two wickets lined up just so, held her breath and swung. Just as the wood mallet hit the wooden ball with a satisfying sound and the ball shot straight through the two wickets, she heard Levi call her name.

"Eve!"

She spun around to see her husband striding toward her, his gait long and purposeful. He did not look pleased. "What are you doing?" When he reached her, he swung around to his brother. "More importantly, what are *you* doing? I'm inside working, waiting on you, and you're out here playing games *with my wife*?"

Tara ran toward them, carrying Eve's blue game ball. "Levi, what's gotten into you?"

Jacob took a step back. "Brother, calm down." He raised both hands, palms out. "I had to go to two stores to find the nails, so it took a while. When I got back, Tara and Eve were trying to—"

"Don't you have work to do inside, Eve?" Levi interrupted loudly.

Eve's first impulse was to lower her head, mumble something apologetic and hurry back to the house. In her father's home, that would have been her response. Otherwise, she might have gotten a berating or, worse, a slap across the face. It happened occasionally. But this man was not her father. He was her husband, and she would not cower. If this marriage was going to work, she needed to make Levi understand what was acceptable and what was not in the life they were building together—that she hoped they would build together. And shouting at her was not acceptable.

She crossed her arms over her chest, met Levi's gaze and said very softly, "You cannot speak to me like that, husband."

For a moment, he stared at her stony-faced, and then suddenly, his expression changed.

Chapter Seven

Levi saw a myriad of emotions on Eve's face. She was scared and angry, but there was also an admirable calm about her. He had caused the first two emotions, but the last was her own. This young woman whom he'd married on impulse was turning out to be so many things he hadn't expected. Initially, that day Mari had led him to the barn, he had offered to marry Eve for her sake. And on some level, he had to admit, at least to himself, that he assumed she would be forever grateful to him, maybe even beholden to him. But in the weeks since that afternoon, no matter what Levi told himself, everything had been about him. Secretly, he had been so proud of the *sacrifice* he had made in marrying this woman. Today it seemed as if it was her sacrifice.

And he was ashamed of himself.

Eve remained where she was, studying him. A lesser woman would have turned to tears and apologies, maybe even fled had her husband behaved as he just had. But not Eve. *Not my wife,* he thought, *because she's a better person than that, a better person than me right now.*

Levi lowered his head. "Eve, I am so sorry," he whispered, unable to meet her gaze.

"Come on," Jacob quietly said to Tara.

"What? Why?" Tara was watching the exchange between Levi and Eve with obvious interest.

Jacob took the croquet mallet and ball from his stepsister's hands, set them in the grass and led her away. Levi watched them go, whispering a silent thanks to his brother. Then he forced himself to meet his wife's gaze.

Eve was dressed in her new ankle-length green dress and a white apron and her feet were bare. She wore her prayer *kapp* over her glossy brown hair that was pinned up, though tendrils had managed to escape. She was watching him with her big, brown eyes.

"Eve, I'm sorry," he said, his voice barely a whisper. He cleared his throat and spoke a little louder. "I know this isn't an excuse, but I was frustrated and angry with my father, and with Jacob. Things aren't going as I had thought they would when I came home and—" He exhaled, ashamed and embarrassed to have behaved so badly. And with his wife, of all people. "I'm sorry," he repeated.

He thought about the words the bishop had spoken the day he and Eve had married.

Likewise, ye husbands, dwell with them according to knowledge, giving honor unto the wife.

He was not honoring his wife, nor was he honoring the sanctity of marriage, family, friendship or any of the things his parents had taught him.

"You're right," he told her, reaching to take her

hands, hoping she wouldn't pull away from him. "I should not have spoken to you that way." He searched her eyes for forgiveness. "And I promise you I'll try very hard to never do it again."

She was quiet for so long that Levi was suddenly afraid he had ruined everything, but at last she spoke in a calm, firm voice.

"Thank you for apologizing, Levi. We all make mistakes. What matters is seeing them and trying to do better." She hesitated and then went on, still allowing him to hold her hands. "Jacob wasn't doing anything wrong except helping me learn how to play the game. He did nothing inappropriate. Jacob would *never* do that. I haven't known him long, but I know what he isn't. And I know that no son Benjamin Miller has raised would ever behave improperly with another man's wife."

"I know," Levi murmured.

"You need to apologize to him, too. And to Tara. We don't want her thinking this is the way married people talk to each other."

Levi nodded. "I'll find them now." Surprised by how good her small hands fit into his, how warm and comforting they were, he was reluctant to let go.

"I think that's a good idea. I'm going back inside to help start supper." She pulled her hands away. "And maybe we can talk about this later?" she asked.

Her gentle face made Levi want to pull her into his arms. But right now, he didn't feel as if he had the right. As her husband, he needed to earn her physical affection. He just had to figure out how.

"Go on, make amends," she told him as she turned to walk away. "They both adore you and look up to you."

"Thank you," Levi called after her.

She glanced over her shoulder and offered a sweet smile. And that smile was what gave Levi the courage to hunt down Jacob and Tara, make his apology and promise to try to be a better big brother.

Levi found Jacob in the buggy shop finishing up applying mud to the last seams on the drywall. Jacob was whistling to himself, obviously content with the task at hand. His younger brother was always so even-tempered, just like his twin, Joshua. Nothing ever seemed to rattle either one, and Levi envied them for that.

"Hey," Levi said.

Jacob glanced over his shoulder. If he was upset with Levi, he didn't look it. "Hey." He returned to his task, smoothing the spackling compound expertly over the taped seams.

"I see you got those last couple drywall nails in."

"*Ya*, the walls look good. We'll let this dry overnight and we can sand in the morning and put the primer I bought on tomorrow afternoon. We'll be done in no time, and then you can get to work building your first buggy."

"It sounds like Eli might be interested in placing an order. With their family growing, he said it's time they got a bigger buggy. I just have to sit down and come up with a price."

"With a family discount," Jacob suggested.

"Of course." Levi took a step toward his brother. "Jacob?"

"*Ya?*"

Levi took a breath, trying to find the right words

to use in an apology to his brother. "Could you stop a second?"

Jacob drew the spackling blade over a nail dimple and then set the spackle and blade down on an aluminum bench they used to reach high on the walls. He turned to his brother.

"I want to tell you how sorry I am." He hooked his thumb in the direction of the house and the front lawn where Jacob and the girls had set up the croquet court. "I don't know what's wrong with me. You weren't doing anything wrong outside with Tara and Eve. You were being nice to my wife." Levi drew the back of his hand across his mouth. "Which is more than I can say for myself."

Jacob was quiet for a moment and then said, "Don't worry about it. I know you're under a lot of stress." He hesitated and then went on. "And I know something's going on between you and Eve."

"What do you mean *going on*?" Levi asked, tempering his tone.

Jacob shrugged. "I can't say for sure. It's not like I'm an expert at marriage or anything."

"No, I don't guess you would be, considering the fact that your chin is clean-shaven."

Jacob met Levi's gaze and went on. "For newlyweds, you two don't seem all that happy together. Eli and Ginger were married months ago and they're still holding hands and grinning at each other all the time."

"As I've said before…" Levi responded, reminding himself that he was the one who had started this conversation. And he had been the one apologizing for words spoken in haste. "…it isn't easy going from being single to having a wife and the responsibility it bears."

"And then coming home with your new wife, staying in the house with *Dat* and Rosemary and the rest of us. I'd guess that's not easy, either." Jacob smiled in understanding. "I just… I'm worried about you. I'm worried about you both. Eve seems like a woman easily content. I guess I'd like to see her that way."

Not sure how to respond, Levi ran his thumbs beneath his suspenders. "I guess these walls aren't going to finish themselves. What do you want me to do? Finish the mudding?"

"*Ne*, I've got this. Grab the nails and put a couple more in that stud near the door," Jacob instructed, pointing to an inside door that opened into a hall their father had created when he'd divided the old dairy barn.

Levi crossed the room to pick up the new box of nails Jacob had brought home from the hardware store. "*Danke*, Jacob," he said quietly.

Jacob picked up his spackling blade. "For what?"

"I don't know. For not being angry with me, I guess. Right now, I don't know that I could bear it."

Jacob squeezed Levi's arm as he passed. "You're going to be fine." He hesitated and then spoke again. "My advice, from a man who fully admits he knows nothing about marriage?"

Levi arched an eyebrow.

"Don't worry about *Dat*. He'll come around, and if he doesn't." He shrugged. "His problem. *Ne*, I think it's best you concentrate on Eve. Because you can change that relationship, and she deserves it. You both do."

* * *

Supper was a quieter affair than usual in the Miller household that night. There were no guests, and Bay and Tara had gone to their sister Lovey's place and stayed for the evening meal.

That afternoon, Tara had taught Eve how to make meatballs and a tomato sauce and they served it over noodles with Parmesan cheese sprinkled on top. They also made fresh garlic bread sticks and a salad from new greens in the garden. Eve not only hadn't known how to make the pasta dish, but she hadn't ever even eaten it. One bite, and she decided that spaghetti might be her favorite meal of all time. The week before, Rosemary had given her some index cards to write down recipes and she intended to add it to her growing stack.

When everyone had had their fill of the meal, there were sweet home-canned peaches covered in cream and sprinkled with cinnamon for dessert. After everyone was properly stuffed, Rosemary took her toddlers upstairs for a bath, and the men drifted out of the room one by one until there was no one left but Tara, Levi and Eve.

As Eve carried a stack of dirty dinner plates to the sink where Tara was already washing, she saw Levi begin to gather glasses from the table. She turned to him. "What are you doing?"

He carried the glasses to the counter, setting them down with the dirty dishes. "Helping."

Eve lifted her brows, confused. She had never once in her life seen her father pick up a dirty dish off the table. Her mother had done it until her death, and then he had left them for his daughters to pick up. "You're helping clean up the kitchen?"

He shrugged. "My *mam* always used to say 'many hands make light work.'"

"Is that from the Bible?" Tara asked, lowering the whole stack of dinner plates into the hot, sudsy water.

"*Ne*, I don't think so." He went back to the table and picked up the can of Parmesan cheese and a jar of home-made salad dressing and carried them to the refrigerator. "It's just something people say."

"Like a proverb," Tara said.

Levi pointed at her. He seemed as if he was in a good mood. "Exactly."

Eve frowned. "I don't understand. Isn't Proverbs a chapter in the Bible?"

"*Ya*, but a proverb can also be a general kind of thing. It can just mean a saying that has a lesson in it," Levi explained, seeming unperturbed by her question. Her father had never appreciated questions of any sort, but he particularly disliked questions that fell into the category of *fancy learning*. Levi's family, however, enjoyed sharing knowledge and even encouraged the children to be inquisitive.

Tara turned from the sink, water dripping from her hands. "It's like an adage."

Eve stared at Tara. "I don't know that word, either. Did you learn that in school?"

She shook her head. "*Ne*, but you know Ethan's a schoolmaster, right? He told me. He reads a lot."

"We like to tease him sometimes about knowing a whole lot of useless information," Levi said and Tara chuckled.

"My father only allowed us to finish the sixth grade," Eve said, collecting silverware from the table. "He saw no need for more schooling than that. At least for girls."

"We all went until we were sixteen in New York." Tara had returned to her dishwashing. "A lot of girls I knew stopped when they were fourteen. I wanted to do the same, but *Mam* wouldn't let me."

Eve carried the silverware to the sink, and Tara took a step back to drop it straight into the sudsy water. "I would love to have gone until I was sixteen. I like to read. At least I used to."

Levi began pushing chairs and benches under the table. "Ethan's got lots of schoolbooks. If you want, I can ask him if we can borrow some. You just have to tell me what kind."

"And that would be all right?" Eve asked her husband, surprised by how open he was to education—especially for women.

"Sure." Levi carried an empty serving bowl stained with red sauce. "Okay if I steal my wife for a little while once we get everything off the table?" he asked his sister.

"Sure. Go now." She glanced around the kitchen. "We're practically done straightening up, and only one of us can wash at a time."

Eve looked to Levi, not sure why he wanted to be alone with her. He hadn't once since they arrived made an effort to spend time with just her. Not that she could blame him. She had been the one who had suggested it the day they had ice cream, and look how that had turned out. Then there had been the incident with Jacob earlier in the day. Eve was beginning to worry that maybe she and Levi just weren't compatible. And then where did that leave them?

"Just us?" Eve asked.

He grinned wryly, reminding her of the man she had admired from afar before she changed both their lives forever with one bad decision. "If you're willing, after my behavior today."

Eve dried her hands on a dish towel. "*Ya*, I'll swing with you," she said, now excited and apprehensive at the same time. "But I… I should help Tara finish the dishes. Dry them and put them away."

He shrugged. "Then we'll do it together and then go outside."

Tara giggled. "Eve, go with him. I can finish here."

Levi headed for the door.

Eve looked at him, at Tara and then back at Levi again.

"Go!" Tara repeated, making a shooing motion. "You're newlyweds. *Mam* says newlyweds need time together without family around."

So Eve followed her husband through the house and out the front door, onto the front porch that she'd never seen anyone use since she'd arrived. Everyone came and went by the back porch, which was more accurately the side of the house. They sat in chairs there, too, sometimes while doing chores like snapping green beans.

"Nice evening," Levi said as he sat down on the swing that was big enough for two or three. "Come on, sit down with me." He patted the rattan seat.

Eve hesitated, suddenly nervous.

"Come on, Eve." He patted the place beside him again. "I won't bite, I promise. After the dressing-down you gave me today, I'm the one who ought to be afraid of you."

She pressed her lips together and sat down on the swing. He gave it a push and she lifted her legs, enjoying the little rush she felt in her chest as they glided forward. The warm evening breeze tickled the pieces of hair that had fallen from the knot at the nape of her neck.

She looked at Levi. "I didn't mean to dress you down."

"*Ya*, you did," he argued. "And I deserved it."

Though they weren't touching, they were close enough that she could feel the warmth of his body. She could smell the Ivory soap he'd used to wash up with before supper. And when she looked at him, he was smiling hesitantly. She liked his beard that was growing in; it made him even more handsome than he already was.

"So… I've been thinking on this matter. I took a walk after I apologized to Tara and Jacob, and I… prayed. I asked God to help me be the husband you deserve, Eve and…" He hesitated and then went on. "I was thinking about what you said about us needing to spend more time together. Because we don't know each other very well. Because we didn't court before we said our vows. And I agree with you. I just wasn't sure how to go about it."

Eve watched his face, trying to figure out where he was going with this conversation.

"But God answered my prayers," he declared.

"He did?"

"*Ya*." He gave the swing another push. "We didn't get to court, so I think we need to court now."

She knitted her brows. "What?"

He leaned back in the swing, sliding his arm across the back so that his fingertips brushed her shoulder. "I'd like to court you, Eve."

She looked at him suspiciously. He wasn't making sense. "But we're married."

"So better you court me than someone else, right?"

When Levi smiled at her the way he was smiling now, she felt a little light-headed and she smiled back shyly. "Okay." She drew out the word. "How are we going to court?"

He rolled his shoulders back. He was wearing a short-sleeved shirt the color of the blue dress she'd ruined escaping from Jemuel.

"We're going to go on dates." He gave a nod of confidence. "We're going to get to know each other. Dates we arrange, not Rosemary," he amended, referring to their trip to the dentist.

"Dates?" she asked, still not quite following.

"Like..." He held up his finger. "I ran into Sara Yoder yesterday at the grain store and she heard I'd married. She asked if you and I would be interested in chaperoning at a supper she's having next weekend. With it being summer, she says it's harder to get folks to help out."

"Sara Yoder." As Eve racked her brain, trying to remember who she was, she gazed out at the front yard. Someone had picked up the croquet mallets and balls and set them next to a tree, ready if anyone wanted to play. "Does she go to our church?" she asked.

"*Ne*, she lives over at Seven Poplars, which is a little north of here. She's the matchmaker."

"A matchmaker?" she asked. She had heard of matchmakers but had never met one. "In Kent County?"

"*Ya*, she came from out west a few years ago. She's a cousin to Hannah Hartman. Hannah is married—"

"To the Amish veterinarian," Eve interrupted excitedly. "I know who she is."

He laughed. "So Tara's gossiping is good for something."

"She wasn't gossiping," Eve said in her new sister's defense. "She's just trying to help me get to know people and how they're related. And actually, it was Ginger who told me first."

"Fair enough," Levi answered. He pushed the swing again and they drifted backward. "Anyway, Sara is expecting a pretty good-sized crowd of young folks and she likes having a little help keeping an eye on everyone. Mostly the guys, to make sure everyone behaves as the bishops would expect."

She nodded, touched that he would not only come up with such a plan but that he was willing to implement it. That he cared enough about the vow he had made to her to try to make things better between them. "I think I'd like to go to Sara Yoder's. With you. On a date."

"Good." He glanced at her. "It'll be fun. And we'll get a chance to be together, away from here. Time to talk."

"And… What other kinds of dates can we go on? Seeing as how we're married."

He shrugged. "We'll just have to be creative. Like… I thought we could take the old rowboat over to the pond and paddle around. Maybe throw a fishing line in."

"I've never been fishing," she said, her interest piqued.

He drew back. "Never been fishing?"

"*Ne*, my brothers went sometimes, down to a creek near our place, but our *dat* didn't think it was any place for a woman."

"I'm not going to get into how your father and I disagree in matters, but I don't see anything wrong with a female of any age fishing. Especially a wife fishing with her husband. So what do you say?"

"I'd like to do that, too. With you," she added, feeling a little shy, but excited at the same time.

"It's a date, then."

Levi picked at a tiny tear in his pants and Eve made a mental note to repair it next time the pants went through the wash.

"But the thing about this," Levi continued, "is that we can't tell anyone that's what we're doing. That we're courting. We don't want them to be suspicious."

"Because they think we knew each other before we married," she said.

"*Ya*, I would assume they do, although truth be told—" he looked away "—I don't know what my father is thinking these days. He's barely talking to me."

"I know he's upset with you because he thinks you took liberties with me. Maybe you should tell him the truth?"

"*Ne,*" he answered firmly. "We agreed no one need know."

"I'm sorry he jumped to that conclusion, Levi," she told him gently.

He looked at her again, a sad smile on his face. "We

both are. But today, taking my walk and praying, I realized that I need to concentrate on what I can change and put everything else in God's hands. Because He always comes through for me."

Chapter Eight

Levi made good on his promise. The following week, after a light supper of sandwiches and salads, Eve and Levi set out through the orchard alone on another date. The thermometer on the back porch read ninety degrees when they left, but there was a nice breeze and the sun, now low in the sky, felt good on Eve's face. She hadn't had a chance all day to get outside except when she'd taken scraps to the chicken house. She and Nettie and Tara had spent hours straightening up a room of the cellar and washing and organizing canning jars in anticipation of putting up tomatoes that were beginning to ripen in the garden.

Swinging a basket on her arm, she glanced up at her husband. There hadn't been an overnight change in their relationship, but since their talk on the front porch swing, it was evident that Levi was going out of his way to get to know her better. With both of them so busy, it was hard to find time alone that wasn't in their bedroom, but he was making an effort. The day before, they had walked the long lane together to get the mail and back, talking the whole way. And a few days before that, Levi had taken her with him to the feed mill to pick up grain in a wagon, and they'd stopped for ice cream cones at Byler's store.

"I didn't know there was a pond on the property," Eve said, enjoying the feel of the warm grass under her bare feet as she walked beside Levi. "How did I not know there was a pond?"

He shifted two fishing poles on his shoulder. "I don't know. I guess it didn't come up. We've got a big piece of property. *Dat* and Rosemary ended up buying two farms side by side. There was no house on the smaller one, just an old house trailer and some chicken houses that were falling down. We bulldozed those over."

"How big is the property?" she asked, hoping she wasn't overstepping her bounds with such personal information about her in-laws. But if she was going to live here, if they were going to make their life together on his father's property, it was only right she know.

"About three hundred acres."

The number shocked Eve. Her father owned ten acres and sold meats at a farmers market to make ends meet. "That's a lot of land," she murmured.

He shrugged. "Not something we advertise."

Obviously, she thought. To talk about owning such a vast piece of property, with no mortgage, would be *hochmut*…arrogant. Prideful, in the wrong way.

"*Dat* and Rosemary both sold their farms in upstate New York to buy it," Levi continued. "They were set on having enough land to go around so that any of their children who wanted to make homes here could."

Eve turned that information over in her head thoughtfully. It seemed like a vast amount of land, especially here in Delaware, where most of the farms were smaller than the ones in the Lancaster area. "So…did Benjamin already give each of you a piece of land?"

"*Ne*. It's up to us to choose once we're married. And ready to build." He glanced at her. "I'm hoping that in a year's time, I'll have sold enough buggies to have the cash to break ground on our home." He offered a smile that almost seemed bashful, which made her smile.

She felt her cheeks grow warm at the thought of living alone with Levi. Right now, she was enjoying life in a big house full of family, a family who loved and respected each other. But with the subtle changes beginning to take place between her and Levi, she suspected that, with time, she would be ready for that next step in their married life. She didn't consciously think about children, but she had the same dream every Amish woman had. She wanted a house full of them, and though she and Levi had not discussed the matter directly, she sensed he wanted the same thing.

"I figure we have time to choose the best spot," Levi went on. "The property fronts on two roads, so we have the option to get a little farther away from the big house and have our own lane if that's what we want."

Eve nodded. "Plenty of time." She looked up at him. "How many buggies do you think you can build in a year? I'm just wondering," she added quickly. "It's not that I'm not content in the big house. I love being a part of a family where everyone works together, gets along together. It's only that I'm curious. I don't know anything about buggy making."

Levi tilted his head one way and then the other. "I

figure the first buggy will take me the longest. I've constructed all of the parts lots of times, but only one buggy from start to finish, and that was a small, open two-seater. Jeb, who I worked for, was always building several buggies at a time. He taught Jehu and me how to do something on one buggy, and then we'd do it on the next on our own. My friend Jehu was the other apprentice. You ever meet him? Jehu Yutzy? From Ohio?"

She shook her head no, switching the basket from one hand to the other. It was beginning to get heavy. She'd packed them a little snack to share in the boat: sweet tea and mini lemon tarts she and Tara had baked.

"Nice guy. Anyway, we learned from Jeb Fisher, but also each other. Jehu's hoping to have his own shop someday, but he doesn't have a *dat* with the finances to help him get going like I do. He'll have to work for someone else and save his money until he can buy the equipment and supplies. Because *Dat* started buggy making as a hobby, he's collected the necessary tools."

"It's good of Benjamin to help you this way. To help us," she added.

"I know, I know." He sighed. "I remind myself of that every day and give thanks to God for his generosity. I just didn't expect him to react the way he has to me marrying."

Eve pressed her lips together. "I'm sorry. I know it's my fault."

Levi stopped, brushing his fingertips against her bare arm. It was so warm outside that she was wearing a short-sleeved dress, a second one Rosemary had made for her, this one in a peach color. Now she had two everyday dresses, so she always had a clean one when the other was in the wash.

"Eve, please don't blame yourself," Levi said. "Remember, I was the one who offered to marry you. You didn't ask me. And no one forced me. It was my choice, and I don't blame you. I would never blame you. This is between me and my *vader. Oll recht?*"

"Oll recht," she repeated, gazing into his gray eyes that were becoming more familiar with each passing day.

He smiled down at her and then cocked his head. "Come on. We better get going. This is the best time of day for fishing, you know."

They began walking again and fell into an easy conversation.

Half an hour later, Eve found herself seated on a wooden bench in a rowboat in the middle of a half-acre pond. Levi had explained to her that the state had helped folks dig them back in the 1960s for emergency water. They dotted the county, providing water so the volunteer fire companies could fight fires better in the rural areas. It was stocked with bass every few years and supported a whole host of animals like frogs and turtles and such. There was even evidence a beaver had tried to take up residence in the cattails on one edge, though Levi said it was long gone by the time they bought the farm.

Eve had already caught two bass. It had been fun to try her hand at fishing, but she'd felt so bad for the live grasshoppers they had used for bait that, after catching two fish, she'd had enough of the sport.

"Do you want to go back to the house?" Levi asked her as he slowly reeled in his line. He'd caught three fish. They had released all of them, as they often did, her husband explained.

She watched his red-and-white plastic bobber bob across the surface of the pond. She'd already reeled her line in, and her pole was lying in the bottom of the boat. She smiled at Levi, sitting in the bow, facing her. "*Ne*, not yet." She folded her hands on her lap, enjoying the slight rocking of the boat. "It's too nice out here. Unless you're ready to go back," she added, hoping he wasn't.

He shook his head. "Nope, I'm enjoying sitting in the middle of a pond on a warm summer evening with my wife."

He was smiling at her, and she couldn't resist smiling back. When he looked at her the way he was looking at her now, she felt warm all over. And...safe. That was the best way to describe it.

Her whole life, she had lived by the whims of her unpredictable father. He had always provided food and heat and some form of clothing, but she had tiptoed around him, never knowing when he would lose his temper. Usually, he just threw things or hit a wall with a fist, but occasionally his hand met with one of his children's faces. Or her mother's. Her mother always had an excuse for his behavior, making it somehow seem all right, but now, living with Levi's family, she knew that it wasn't.

No, actually she'd realized that the morning she had come home after Jemuel had tried to attack her. When her father had not protected her from that horrible man, she saw him for the terribly flawed man he was.

Not that Levi wasn't flawed. He was impatient some-times. But she had never felt physically threatened by him. And now, as the days passed, she was beginning to feel more and more comfortable with her husband. Not only was she learning that she liked him but, in her heart of hearts, she knew he would always protect her. As he had the day he had offered to marry her.

Eve felt herself blush and glanced over the rowboat's side to watch a water strider glide across the surface, barely creating a ripple. "Don't look at me that way," she told Levi bashfully.

"What way?" He set his pole in the bottom of the boat and pushed up the brim of his straw hat in an ex-aggerated motion, as if to get a better look at her. "A man can't look at his pretty wife?"

She giggled, shaking her head as if he had said the silliest thing. No one had ever called her pretty before, not even her mother. She knew it wasn't true, but it still made her feel good inside. "Are you thirsty? Would you like iced tea?"

"I would."

She reached for the basket behind her. "I brought some fruit tarts, too."

"I was wondering what smelled so amazing in that basket."

Eve pulled out a pint jar of iced tea, the glass wet with condensation, and handed it to him.

Levi unscrewed the Ball jar lid and took a sip. "What a clever way to bring drinks. Doesn't spill a drop." He took a big gulp and exhaled loudly. "*Goot.* Just the way I like it. Not too much sugar, but still sweet, and lemony."

"We bought a whole bag of lemons at Walmart the

other day." She lifted a square plastic dish from the basket, removed its lid and held the container out to him.

He leaned over, and his eyes got wide. "Lemon tarts!" He lifted one out of the container and held it up. "That might be the prettiest tart I've ever seen. It looks like something you'd buy in an Englisher bakery." He looked up at her. "What's the decoration on top?"

She took a tart for herself and leaned forward to set the container beside Levi on the bench. "Lemon zest," she said, fighting a feeling of pride that tightened in her chest. She liked cooking for Levi. She liked making things for him that he enjoyed.

"Zest?" he asked. Then he took a big bite of the tart, and the crust was so perfect that it flaked but didn't crumble in his hand. "I don't know that word."

"It's the peel, but just the yellow part." She nibbled on the crust of her tart. "The white is bitter."

Levi finished his tart in three more bites and reached for another, closing his eyes in pleasure. "So good," he murmured. "I might have to have a third."

"You can have the rest." She dared to meet his gaze. "I made them for you, Husband."

"I like hearing you call me that."

Not knowing what to say, she glanced away, reaching for her iced tea.

"Wanna play a game?" Levi asked, taking another tart.

"A game?"

He shrugged one shoulder. He was wearing a blue shirt, and it made his eyes look even bluer. "Sort of a game," he said. "Let's take turns asking each other questions, then we both have to answer."

"Questions like what?"

He chewed thoughtfully. "Like…what's your favorite animal?"

"My favorite animal?" She laughed. "Do you mean to eat?"

He laughed with her. "*Ne*, like what animal did you always like as a child? It could be a barnyard animal, or something exotic."

"Like a tiger," she suggested, wide-eyed. Of course, she had never seen a tiger, but she had seen pictures of them.

"Exactly." He wiped at some crumbs in the corner of his mouth with the back of his hand, and she pulled a cloth napkin from the basket and tossed it onto his lap. "I'll go first," he offered, using the napkin. "Easy. Mine is an alpaca."

"An alpaca?" She laughed, relieved she knew the animal. He was so much better educated than she was that she feared he'd name a creature she hadn't known even existed.

"*Ya*, alpacas. When I was learning to read, we had this book in school that had a letter and picture on every page, and the A page was my favorite because it had an alpaca on it. My teacher had to explain to me what it was. And then my *dat* took me to a farm to see some. Some Englisher he knew raised them for their wool."

Eve nodded, fascinated. She had never had anyone in her life who would have taken her to see an alpaca.

"I'd love to have an alpaca of my own someday. I know someone here in Kent County who has them," he told her excitedly. "An Amish guy. Have you ever seen one?"

She shook her head.

"Then I'm going to take you to see them," he declared.

"Who has alpacas?" She sipped her tea. The ice had all melted, but it was still nice and cool.

"Our veterinarian. Albert Hartman."

She pointed at Levi. "*Recht.* He became Amish to marry…" She couldn't remember the woman's name.

"Hannah," Levi said. "That's right. Let's plan to go see Albert's alpacas soon. For one of our dates, maybe. Would you like that?"

"I would," she told him.

"Okay, so what's yours?" he asked.

"Chipmunks. They're so small and cute, and I love how they race around," she told him. "I just love chipmunks. But not to eat, mind you."

He drew back, laughing. "I would hope not." They laughed together, and he said, "Okay, your turn. Ask me a question. Anything."

She thought for a moment, then asked, "Favorite cookie?"

He grimaced. "A hard one. Let's see…oatmeal cookies, made with chocolate chips, not raisins. Not that I don't like raisins in my cookies, but I love chocolate."

"I love chocolate in my oatmeal cookies, too!" she told him excitedly, thinking that would be easy to remember.

They bounced four or five more questions between them, and then Levi said, "Favorite color?" Before she could answer, he put up his hand. "Wait, wait. Let me guess." He squeezed his eyes shut for a moment, then opened them. "Blue?"

She smiled with a nod. "How did you know?"

Their laughter died away. "A guess. You said it was your mother's favorite color. And you told me you ruined your dress...that night."

Surprisingly, his mention of the night Jemuel had tried to attack her didn't upset her. Instead, she was touched that he remembered the dress and why it had been distressing to lose it.

"And your favorite color?" she asked, studying his handsome face.

He pressed his hands to his knees and leaned closer to her. "Blue."

"That's always been your favorite color, too?" she asked suspiciously.

His gaze never left hers as he shook his head slowly. "Not always. But it is now." He smiled and she felt a flutter in her chest. "Because it's yours, wife."

Eve was so excited to meet the matchmaker Sara Yoder on their next date that the buggy had barely rolled to a stop, and she was climbing down. This was her and Levi's first invitation as a married couple to serve as chaperones and she was thrilled to be asked. She'd never served as a chaperone, so she didn't know exactly what it entailed, but how hard could it be? she wondered. A chaperone's responsibility was to make sure single men and women behaved according to the *ordung*, rules established by the church.

It seemed to her that it would be especially simple to keep their eye on folks in a place like Seven Poplars, where Old Order Amish didn't practice *rumspringa*, and there were plenty of organized activities to keep them from exploring dangerous temptations like drugs, alcohol and premarital relations. Not that she was so naive as to think those failings didn't exist among the Amish in any community, but like Hickory Grove, Tara had told her that "everyone in Seven Poplars mostly behaved."

Levi got down from the buggy on the other side to tie up the bay to a hitching post as Eve looked around. Though they had arrived early, there were already several wagons and buggies parked. There was no activity around the house and no sounds in the barnyard, except for the lowing of a cow in the pasture in the distance and the bleat of goats she couldn't see.

Everyone was already at the hospitality barn, she supposed.

"Excited?" Levi asked, flashing her a smile.

"Ya." Eve beamed, looking down at the new canvas sneakers she'd bought at Spence's Bazaar for the event. Levi had generously given her fifty dollars to spend when she went with Tara and Nettie the day before. It had been more than enough to buy a nice pair of summer shoes, but when she'd tried to return the change, he'd told her to keep it. "Every woman needs a little pin money, don't they?" he'd asked her.

"I've never seen a hospitality barn," Eve told Levi. "That's what Tara said Sara called it."

Levi checked a strap on the horse's harness and then came around the hitching post to her. "I've never heard of it before, either. But if there's one thing I know about Sara Yoder, it's to expect the unexpected."

"What does that mean?" she asked, smiling because he was smiling.

"You'll see," he answered.

Eve walked beside her husband, and side by side, they followed a path that ran between the barn where Sara housed her animals and a long shed that looked to have been enclosed recently. A sign with writing burned into a large piece of wood hung over a door and read Bunkhouse.

"Tara said Sara was widowed." Eve hurried along eagerly. "She said Sara makes her living from match-making. Did she build this hospitality barn for her business?"

"Sort of. She had it *rebuilt*. When Sara first moved here from somewhere out west, she purchased it for practically nothing because it was about to be torn down at its original location to make room for a subdivision. With the help of friends and neighbors, a construction crew dismantled the barn and then rebuilt it here."

As they walked beyond the barnyard, the path opened into a grassy field blooming with black-eyed Susans. There, what had to be the hospitality barn came into view. Eve halted to admire it, planting her hands on her hips. It was a picture-perfect gambrel-roofed building with a metal roof, red siding and jaunty rooster weather vane perched high on a white cupola. Double white doors were thrown open, and the sound of voices drifted from inside to mingle with insect song and the peepers.

"Tara said single men and women stay here with Sara?" Eve asked.

They began walking again. "*Ya*. A few at a time, mostly those folks coming from far away. Girls sleep in the house, and while Sara did have boys sleeping in the barn for a while, she just had that shed renovated."

"The one that said 'bunkhouse'?"

He nodded. "And here we are." They walked through the open doors. "I imagine we'll eat inside and wander outside. I saw what looks to be the makings of a bonfire along the side of the barn." Levi looked at her. "Maybe we can roast some marshmallows and make s'mores." His gray eyes twinkled. "I love s'mores. You?"

She laughed. "I know what they are, but I've never had one."

"Never had one?" he gasped, bringing his hand to his chest. He was wearing the new short-sleeve shirt she had made him. It was grass green and she had to admit, he looked rather handsome in it. "Well, we'll right that wrong tonight for sure, wife."

Inside the hospitality barn, Eve gazed around at the interior, taking in the high ceiling, the massive wooden beams and the spotless whitewashed walls. Not only had the inside of the building been insulated, but the old wood floor had been sanded and refinished. Two enormous woodstoves stood in opposite corners, cold now, but she imagined they would make the barn cozy and warm in the winter. Tara had said that Sara used it year-round and was now holding weddings there, as well.

The space was a beehive of activity. Men and boys set up long tables and arranged chairs while women in Amish *kapps* and starched white aprons carried in large stainless steel containers and placed them on counters along one wall.

"Levi!" A short, sturdy, middle-aged woman waved them toward the food area.

"And that is Sara," Levi told Eve.

Sara Yoder was tidy in a blue dress, black stockings and shoes, and a white apron. Her dark textured hair was pinned up into a bun and covered with a starched white prayer *kapp*. And her skin was the color of caramel, still warm in the pan.

Eve had never seen a black Amish woman before.

Levi and Eve walked toward her.

"So this is your bride?" Sara announced with open arms, her dark eyes sparkling.

"Eve," Levi introduced. "And Sara," he told Eve.

"Congratulations on your marriage!" Sara sang, taking Eve's hand between hers. "You married a good man."

Eve felt her cheeks grow warm and she smiled. "That I have," she said, glancing at her husband.

"And I was thrilled when Levi sent word that you could chaperone tonight. I'm bursting at the seams with men and women staying with me, and half the singles in the county are coming tonight. It seems as if love is in the air. I've made two matches this week," she added under her breath.

"Have you?" Eve couldn't imagine what it would be like to hire a matchmaker to find a husband. How could a stranger choose a spouse for a man or a woman? The idea was certainly unconventional. But then it wasn't any more unconventional than how she and Levi ended up married, was it?

Sara opened her arms wide again. "What do you think of my hospitality barn?"

Eve laughed. "You can hardly call it a barn. It's beautiful."

This building was nothing like the barns Eve had ever been inside; some had smelled of hay and animal feed, but others were not so pleasant. She shuddered involuntarily, remembering her father's dank and forbidding stable, all shadows, cobwebs and sagging doors and windows. The place had always smelled of rodents. Eve had spent many mornings and evenings there milking the cows in the semidarkness, and it wasn't a memory that she cared to linger over.

Levi pushed his straw hat back off his head a bit. "I know you have plenty to do, Sara, so we won't keep you. How can we help?"

"Well, once everyone gets here, I just need you, Levi, to keep an eye on the young men. If you see a group of them wandering off, you can pretty much assume they're up to no good. Obviously, no drinking of alcohol is allowed, and the same goes for cigarette smoking. I won't have it. And no fighting," she added. "A couple of weeks ago, I had two get into a fight over who was going to carry a cup of lemonade to a new girl who'd just arrived from Michigan."

"And what can I do?" Eve asked, clasping her hands together.

"Keep an eye on my girls. I can't be everywhere at once. Young women can be naive. They don't understand how easily they can put themselves at risk with a boy they don't know. I thoroughly vet anyone coming to stay with me, but any single in the county is welcome to my events and I can't speak for the character of everyone's cousin's friend."

Eve lowered her gaze. She knew Sara had no knowledge of the details of her marriage to Levi, but the matchmaker's warning about the innocence of young women struck home. If she'd had a woman like Sara in her life, would she have known better than to have gotten into a buggy with Jemuel?

"I think we can handle the chaperoning. What can we do now?" Levi asked.

Sara glanced around. Everyone there seemed to have a task and was getting to it. "Let's see... Would you mind going outside to check to see if we have enough wood for the bonfire? I asked Lem, a nice, shy boy just arrived from Kentucky. He said he would see to it, but he appears to have found something more important to do." She indicated with her chin and Eve followed Sara's line of sight.

A nice-looking young man with a head of white-blond hair and a big grin was taking an armful of paper plates from a short, round woman who looked like she could have been Eve's twin. Seeing the good-looking boy fawning over the plain, chubby girl made her heart sing. Her mother had always said that there was some-one for everyone in God's world. Eve guessed she had been right.

"I can take care of that," Levi told Sara.

"What can I do?" Eve piped up.

"No doubt, there's still work to be had in the kitchen. We're having burritos tonight, so there's a lot of prep work."

"There's a *kitchen* in your barn?" Eve asked.

"Right through that doorway." She pointed. "Every hospitality barn needs a kitchen, don't you think? You can go help if you like. I know there are still tomatoes and cilantro from my garden to be chopped up for the salsa."

Levi turned to Eve. "You okay in here while I see to the firewood?"

She smiled up at him. "Of course."

She watched him go and then turned back to Sara. "So, what exactly is a hospitality barn?" More Amish were coming into the building now, and two teenage girls in black prayer *kapps* were spreading the tables with white tablecloths. "I've never heard of such a thing."

"That's because I made it up myself. I wanted someplace larger than my home where I could get young people together," Sara explained. "For my matchmaking, so that men and women of courting age could meet. Also, our church community needed a safe place to hold youth meetings, singings and frolics. This barn was an answer to our prayers, and it practically fell into my lap. It's more than a hundred years old and is in wonderful shape."

"But the expense of moving the structure." Eve looked around, still in awe.

"A bargain at any price. A lot of Amish communities have problems with their teenagers and young adults being lured into bad habits by the free ways of the English. Even Amish kids need somewhere away from adults to let down their hair, so to speak."

Eve nodded in agreement.

"On Wednesday evenings, Seven Poplars' youth group, the Gleaners, meets here. They do game nights, birthday parties and work frolics here, as well. It's good that Amish children learn the value of work and responsibility, but boys have a lot of energy. If we can positively channel that energy, the entire community benefits."

"Sure seems nice." Eve smoothed her skirt. "Nothing like this where I grew up. Singings and frolics were always at people's homes, the same as when my *mam* grew up."

"Tradition is good." Sara nodded thoughtfully. "It's served our faith well for hundreds of years, but as I see it, we don't live in a vacuum. We have to be open to change when it can be done without endangering our way of life."

"Sara!" A young woman carrying one of the big stainless tubs called from across the room. "Did you want the fixings on this table or that one?" With both hands occupied, she had to use her foot to point.

"I'd better take care of this before we have eight pounds of shredded cheese on the floor," Sara said as she walked away, squeezing Eve's arm.

Eve glanced around the airy barn one more time and then found her way back to the kitchen that was as well equipped as any in an Amish house. There were two large gas cookstoves, two cavernous sinks, a large refrigerator and counters along two walls, as well as an enormous prep island. A slender red-haired woman she didn't know was standing at a big gas stove, stirring sizzling ground beef in several cast-iron frying pans. "Ah, reinforcements have arrived," the woman announced when she spotted Eve. "Want to stir this beef? My hand is about to drop off."

Eve hurried to the stove, introducing herself as she accepted the spoon, and she and her new friend, Lena, were soon chatting as they worked. The next hour was a whirlwind of activity as Eve joined the other women to make and get the fixings out on the buffet table. There were trays of flour tortillas, ground beef, shredded chicken, lettuce, tomato, cheese, pinto beans and rice. They also set out jars of homemade salsa and tubs of sour cream. By the time all the food was on the table and a silent grace had been said, Eve was nearly starving.

She was just adding a serving spoon to a stainless steel tub of pinto beans when she heard Levi behind her. "There you are. I've been looking for you."

She stepped away from the buffet table where folks were lining up, wiping her hands on her apron. "Sara is very organized, but there was still a lot to be done."

"It looks delicious." Levi glanced over her shoulder, checking out the food. "Want to get in line?"

Eve nodded enthusiastically. "I've never had a burrito before."

"Never had a burrito?" He feigned shock.

She shook her head. "You eat so many Englisher foods here in Delaware," she said, thinking of the spaghetti and meatballs and pork medallion stir-fry Tara had taught her to make.

"Is that a bad thing?" he asked.

"*Ne*. I like trying new foods."

"Then come on." He took her hand. "Let's see what you think of beef and bean burritos."

A short time later, Eve held a paper plate with her very first burrito on it, as well as a pile of corn chips covered in gooey yellow cheese. Levi stood beside her, gazing over the crowd, looking for a place for them to sit.

"Wow, there must be fifty or sixty people here," he remarked. "I don't see two seats together." He hesitated. "Wait. How about over there, near the front door?"

She looked in that direction, but there were no dining tables set up. "Where?"

"That little table against the wall." He indicated a card-sized table with a couple of pillar candles and empty glass vases.

She pursed her lips. "No chairs." Her gaze drifted to the long tables packed with young men and women. Everyone seemed to be talking at once, voices and laughter ringing out in the barn. "Do you think, as chaperones, we should be sitting with Sara's guests?"

He looked down at her. "I don't think a matchmaker will object to newlyweds having supper alone together."

She smiled, feeling shy, but pleased. "And we are on a date."

"We are." He tilted his head in the direction of the little table. "Let's put our food down and get bottles of pop." They walked together, plates in their hands. "Root beer, cola or orange?"

"Definitely root beer," she told him.

"Me, too!" He smiled down at her, and his voice grew husky. "Know something?"

"What?" she asked, looking up.

"I like you, Eve."

She nibbled on her lower lip, looking up at him. "You do?"

He nodded, and she felt a warmth wash over her as she thought to herself, *I sure could get used to dating my husband.*

Chapter Nine

Eve veered off the dusty lane, taking the path that led to the side of the vast dairy barn where Levi now spent his days building his first buggy. When they'd arrived in Hickory Grove, he'd been so eager to get started. Looking back, she knew now that his frustration concerning not working—and therefore not earning money—had added to his bad behavior. That and his father's reaction to the unannounced marriage. Now that he was working, he seemed so much better. Levi's relationship with his father still wasn't what it had been before the marriage, but it seemed to her that it was better.

Enjoying her time outdoors, she swung the basket she carried on the crook of her arm, watching dragonflies float lazily in front of her. Someone had mowed the orchard that morning, and even from a distance, Eve could smell the sweet scent of cut grass. It was a perfect summer day.

Her thoughts drifted to the evening before when she and Levi had sat on the edge of her bed and chatted. She smiled at the memory. They hadn't spoken about anything of importance, just their day, but Levi had commented to her how much he looked forward to coming to bed each night because he knew she would be there. He had complimented her on what a good listener she was, and his words had made her heart sing.

After praying together, they had sat side by side for a long moment, looking into each other's eyes. Levi had been silent for so long that she had gotten the impression he'd wanted to say something more, do something, but then he had risen suddenly, and they had said their good-nights. Long after Eve had heard her husband's rhythmic breathing, she had lain awake thinking about how warm and safe she had felt sitting beside Levi. How now, whenever she saw him, she felt a light-headedness that nearly made her giddy.

Was this love? she wondered. Was that what she was feeling? She didn't know because she'd never been in love.

She had, of course, loved, but that was different. She had loved her mother; she loved her brothers and sisters. She knew what that kind of love felt like, but this, this feeling in her chest, it was different. It excited her and scared her at the same time.

It was times like this that she missed her mother the most. Because if her mother had still been alive, she could have asked her about the love between a man and a woman, what it felt like—but her *mam* wasn't here so she had no one to ask. Tara had become a dear friend, but she was still unmarried and had never even had a boyfriend, so Eve couldn't talk to her about these feelings bubbling up inside her. Besides, for all Eve knew,

Tara thought they had fallen in love and that was why they had married.

And Eve couldn't talk to Levi about it. She would be too embarrassed, especially because she didn't know how he felt about her. He had told her several times over the last couple of weeks that he liked her, and she was pleased by that. And she certainly liked him. Liking the man you married seemed like an important part of a good marriage, she thought.

But she wasn't naive enough to think that all Amish marriages were love matches. She knew that from watching other married couples. Men and women wed because it was expected of them by their community, because they wanted children and it was God's way. Sometimes matches were arranged by parents; sometimes two friends or even two strangers just agreed to marry because it was logical. Maybe a widowed man needed a mother for his children, or a woman needed a home of her own.

While knowing all that, secretly, Eve had dreamed of falling in love with a man and marrying him. Her marriage to Levi hadn't happened that way, but what if God gave them the gift of falling in love *after* they married?

Was that too much to hope for? To pray for? she wondered.

Reaching the buggy shop, Eve held tightly to her basket and peered in through the large, open bay door. She heard the loud, grumbling sound of a gas-powered generator. "Levi?" she called, unable to see anything because the bright sunlight was behind her. She stepped inside. *"Hallo?"*

As her eyes adjusted to the light, she saw her husband

leaning over a sawhorse, sanding something. Afraid she might startle him if she approached, she raised her voice. "Levi!"

He looked up, then when he saw it was her, he broke into a grin. He flipped a switch on the electric sander attached to the generator and then turned it off.

"Eve! I didn't think I'd see you until supper," he said, looking at her through a pair of clear safety glasses.

"Nice glasses," she teased as he approached her.

He chuckled and removed them. "My old boss was a stickler for safety. Jehu and I used to complain to each other all the time, but now that I'm my own boss, I see the value in it. I've even got *Dat* wearing them." He set the glasses on a workbench that was covered with parts for a buggy, she guessed, though she couldn't identify any of them. "Tara let you out of the kitchen?" he teased.

"Only for a few minutes." She nibbled on her lower lip, enjoying the back-and-forth with him. "We picked more tomatoes this morning, so we have more to can."

He nodded. "I see. You bring me something?" He pointed to the basket.

"Ya." She swung it on her arm, smiling up at him.

"I hope it's not a jar of canned tomatoes." He held up his hand that had little bits of sawdust on it, palm out. "Don't get me wrong. I love tomatoes fresh on a salad, or in a soup or spaghetti sauce, but I'm not much for eating them out of the jar."

She laughed, loving that he could be playful. "I brought you some limeade."

"Limeade?" His face lit up. "We usually only get lemonade around here."

She set the basket down on a workbench and dug

into it. "Limes were on sale at Byler's store. We bought a big bag of them." She held up a pint canning jar with a screw-top lid.

Levi accepted it, unscrewed the lid and took a big drink. "Mmm, that's good," he muttered.

She smiled at him. "And I brought cookies, too."

"Cookies!" He took another drink. "What kind?"

"Our favorite." She pulled a plastic container from the basket.

"Oatmeal?" he guessed.

"Oatmeal with chocolate chunks. I cut up chocolate bars." She pulled off the lid and offered the container to him.

He took one, reached for another and drew back his hand. "Okay if I have another?"

She laughed. "They're all for you."

"*Ne*, I can't eat all of these cookies," he told her, setting down the jar of limeade after he took a second cookie.

He stepped closer to her, and she smelled the fresh sawdust on him and the underlying scent of his skin that she'd come to associate with her husband. When he met her gaze, she felt the same dizziness she often experienced now whenever he was around.

"One for you, one for me," he told her, offering one of her cookies.

She accepted it and they both bit into them at the same time.

"Best cookie ever," he told her, closing his eyes in pleasure.

"I sprinkle a pinch of salt on the top of each one, just as they come out of the oven," Eve explained.

"Never heard of that. Maybe that's why they're better than Tara's." He opened his eyes. "But please don't tell her that."

"Of course not." She was smiling so big that she could barely chew her cookie. "I would never want to hurt Tara's feelings. She's been so sweet to me since I got here. Like a sister."

"She's a sweet kid," he agreed, taking another cookie from the container.

"Not exactly a kid anymore," Eve told him, looking down at something rubbing against her bare ankle. It was a fluffy white cat.

"Snowball," Levi told her, pushing the rest of the cookie into his mouth. "A rescue. Ethan brought her home when she was just a little thing. Jacob took over her care. He loves strays."

Eve leaned over and petted the cat. "I like cats."

"Me, too." He hooked his thumb in the direction of the workbench covered in buggy parts. "Want to see what I'm doing?" he asked. Then he shook his head, grimacing. "Probably not, right?"

"I would love to see what you're doing." He moved toward the workbench and she followed him. "I keep wanting to come down to the barn to see what you do, but I don't want to bother you."

"Never think you're a bother, Eve. I wish you'd come down to the shop more often. Especially if you bring me cookies." He hesitated. "You want to see what I'm working on right now?"

She nodded excitedly.

"Okay." He started to lead her over to where he'd been working, then turned. "Wait. I almost forgot. We had a big delivery this morning and I have something for you."

"For me?" she whispered. "What?"

"A gift," he said, walking over to a large stack of cardboard boxes in various shapes and sizes. He moved several small boxes, picking up one and then the other to read the return addresses. "Ah ha!" he declared. "Here it is." He turned around and offered it to her.

"What is it?" she asked, staring at the box she'd accepted from him.

He tucked his hands behind his back. "Guess you'll have to open and see."

Eve hesitated, trying to extend the moment. She'd only ever received a couple of gifts in her whole life, and they had been from her mother when she was a child.

"Open it," he encouraged.

She set it on a pile of boxes and opened it. Inside was a brown paper bag and inside of that, something soft. She looked up to see him smiling, then gently slid the gift from the bag.

It was yards of a blue cotton blend fabric, and she knew exactly what it was for. And she was touched by his kindness in a deep place in her heart that she hadn't even known existed until now. *"Danke,"* she managed when she found her voice.

"It's for a dress. For you," he told her. "Blue, because it's your favorite color."

She looked up at him, clutching the fabric to her chest, her eyes glistening. "You remembered."

"After I ordered it, I asked Rosemary to make you the dress, but she suggested I give you fabric first. She said it would mean more to you that way. And she thought you might like to make it yourself. Because it came from me," he explained.

"She was right." Eve gently slid the fabric back into the bag and placed it in her basket. "Such a kind thing to do. But I don't want you to think I need things bought for me."

"I think nothing of the sort. I'm just glad you like it." He tipped his head in the direction of his work area. "Still want to see what I'm doing?"

"Of course," she told him, setting down the basket to follow him.

Grinning, Levi began explaining to her what he was working on: the chassis of the buggy. He explained to her how the chassis was the frame beneath the buggy the wheels were attached to and then showed her the long, wooden reaches he was sanding that would connect the front and rear axles on the chassis.

He chattered on about head blocks, spring bars and shaft couplings, and as he talked, Eve's thoughts kept drifting. As Levi spoke, she admired how handsome he was and how, when he smiled, his whole face lit up and she couldn't help but smile back at him. She still couldn't believe he had given her a gift, and such a perfect gift. Now she would have a blue dress that would remind her every day of her mother. And of the kindness of the man she had married. When they had first arrived in Hickory Grove, Eve had worried she had made a mistake in marrying Levi, but she knew now that it hadn't been.

Levi kept talking and she tried to pay attention.

When he led her to a workbench to show her the parts of the drum brakes he was putting together, his hand brushed hers as he passed her parts to show her how they went together. The brakes of a buggy, he explained, kept the buggy from running into the horse when you pulled back on the reins.

Eve swallowed hard. His hand was warm and rough in the places where he had calluses, and she wondered what it would be like to hold it. To walk together, holding hands. She had rarely seen Amish men and women holding hands, but Rosemary and Benjamin did. Every other Sunday, when they walked to church, they went separately from their big, blended family. They walked close together, holding hands, talking and laughing. Eve wondered if it was too much to hope for, to someday hold hands with Levi on their way to church.

Levi stopped midsentence and stared at her.

Eve wondered if he was waiting for her to answer a question. She'd been so lost in her own foolish dreaming that she hadn't been listening.

"This is boring," he declared, throwing up his hand. "I'm boring you."

"Ne." She shook her vehemently. "You're not. I want to know what you do. I like hearing about it, even if…if I don't understand everything. My day is so boring— cooking, cleaning, hanging clothes on the line. Not that I mind," she added quickly. "I like being useful. But what you do—" She gazed around his shop that was stacked with cardboard boxes full of parts he had ordered and benches covered in parts in various stages of assembly. "This is so much more exciting," she declared enthusiastically.

When Eve met his gaze, she realized he was staring

at her. "What?" she asked, wiping her mouth, afraid she had cookie crumbs on it.

He shook his head, taking a step closer to her. He was smiling. "Nothing, I just… It's all I can do to talk when you're standing so close because I…" He reddened. "I keep thinking that I'd like to kiss you, Eve."

She blushed and looked down at her bare feet that had gotten dusty on the walk over. Suddenly her heart was pounding. "I… I've never kissed a man," she heard herself say.

Levi took another step and stood in front of her. "I don't want to be forward." His voice had become husky.

Realizing he was as nervous as she was, Eve relaxed and giggled. "We're married, Levi. You have a right to kiss me."

He lifted his gaze. Held hers. "Would you like to kiss me, Wife?"

Not trusting herself to speak, she nodded. Then she closed her eyes and waited.

Eve didn't know what she expected, but when he wrapped his arms around her and brushed his lips ever so gently across hers, she felt enveloped in a warmth she had never felt before. In his embrace, she felt safe and content and…and cared for, if not loved.

Levi kissed her and she opened her eyes to see him studying her. "How was that?" he asked.

She raised her hand to touch her lips. "Warm and tingly," she told him with a shy smile. "How was it for you?"

Still holding her in his arms, he chuckled. "*Goot.* You smell like vanilla."

She stepped back. "Probably spilled some on myself," she told him, laughing as she ran her hand over her apron.

He was still studying her. "I don't think so."

"*Ach*, I should get back to the house," she said, feeling awkward. And excited. She would never have believed it could happen, that a handsome, smart, capable man like Levi could fall in love with a plain wren like her, but suddenly, she saw that possibility. And all she could think was *God is good*. "Tara will wonder what happened to me."

"*Ya*, you'd best go. We wouldn't want her coming down here looking for you and finding us kissing." He raised an eyebrow, his tone teasing.

"*Ya*... I mean, *ne*!" She shook her head, vehemently. "We wouldn't want that."

They stood looking at each other for a long moment and then Levi said softly, "Wife, you best get going, else I'm liable to kiss you again."

She covered her mouth with her hand to stifle another giggle and turned and hurried out of the barn, grabbing her basket with the fabric as she went.

"Eve!" Levi called after her. "You forgot the cookies."

"They're all for you!" she called over her shoulder. Then she hurried back up the lane to the house, feeling as if she might burst with joy.

On a Sunday morning, Eve walked beside Levi along the road, headed toward his brother Ethan's home. They were both in their Sunday best, her in her black dress, crossed cape and bonnet, him in black pants, a white shirt and black vest, his wide-brimmed black felt hat on his head. His beard was coming in nicely, making him all the more handsome. Some husbands let their beards grow without trimming them, leaving them to look unkempt, but not Levi. For a man who worked with his hands, he was fastidious about cleanliness. No matter what he did on the farm, whether it was muck horse stalls or work in the buggy shop, when he came to the supper table, his hands and nails were meticulously scrubbed, and his face was freshly washed.

Pride swelled in her chest. With every passing day, she was surer of her impulsive decision to marry Levi. They were still getting to know each other, but as July slipped into August, she became more assured of her choice. As she began to feel more confident in their growing relationship, she was finding the desire in her heart to forgive Jemuel for what he had done. She prayed for him every day now because it was the right thing to do. But also because, had he not done what he had, maybe she would never have ended up where she was now, safe and happy.

"I hope you baked plenty of brownies." Levi touched his hand to her shoulder as they moved farther off the road to allow a motorcycle to fly by.

"I made three pans. They're in the wagon with Bay, and the girls took them to Marshall and Abigail's this morning." They had left early, with the children, to help their sister-in-law with last-minute preparations to host church. Eve had been invited to go with them, but she had stayed behind to clean up the breakfast dishes. Her offer hadn't been entirely selfless. She had remained so that she could walk with Levi to church. While bad weather or distance required families to take buggies to

Sunday services, Benjamin preferred his family walk when possible. Which was just fine with Eve because it gave her time alone with Levi. Rather than walking with the family, they had fallen into the habit of making the trek alone together, as Benjamin and Rosemary often did.

"We made three pans of scalloped potatoes, too," she went on. "And four dozen buttermilk biscuits."

"Buttermilk biscuits!" Levi exclaimed as they moved closer to the road so they didn't have to walk in the tall weeds. "I love buttermilk biscuits. They're my favorite."

Eve looked at him quizzically. "Yesterday you said cheddar was your favorite."

"Can't I have two favorites?"

She rolled her eyes. The amount of food her husband could eat in a day astounded her. And yet he never gained a pound. She looked at a buttermilk biscuit and could feel it going to her hips. "Why are you worried about how much food we brought? There's always more than enough to go around when we break for the midday meal on Sundays."

"It's going to be a long day," he told her, walking slowly so she could keep up. "I heard *Dat* discussing it with Ethan last night. He didn't say anything to me about it," he added quietly.

Eve took his hand and squeezed it, knowing it pained him that his relationship with his father remained strained. She was still shy about their physical affection for each other, but she found it easier out of sight of anyone else. And she wanted to comfort him.

"We'll be talking today about splitting up our district after the first service. After we eat, the afternoon service will be shortened, and the plan will be announced, then discussed."

Eve's eyes widened. Hickory Grove had been abuzz with the topic for weeks. Everywhere she went, to Byler's store, to Ginger's quilting circle, to Spence's Bazaar, the women were talking about it and what it would mean to each family, the positives and the negatives. "So we're definitely splitting the district?"

"*Ya*. The elders have decided it's time. Past time. We've gotten so big that we can only meet in the larger homes. A church isn't meant to get so big that we can't meet in any member's home. We each have to take our turn and share the responsibility."

"So we'll have a new bishop?" she asked, thinking how much she liked Bishop Simon.

"*Ne*, Bishop Simon offered to take the new district, but we'll be choosing men to become preachers and deacons from the new congregation." He took her hand, threading his fingers through hers. "The older district will choose a new bishop from our preachers."

"I see," Eve said.

"I talked to Ethan after *Dat* left for home. Ethan said *Dat* was the first from the oldest, most established families to offer to join the new district. The division is sort of based on where we live, but it's important that families who have been here a while join the new district, too. Ethan thought he and Abigail would be going with us, as well as Joshua and Phoebe and Ginger and Eli, but Lovey and Marshall will be staying with our old district. Just because of where they live."

"Will Rosemary be upset, not getting to see her daughter and grandchildren on Sundays?"

"Both districts will be on the same schedule, so even though we meet in different places for services, visiting Sundays will be the same."

She nodded thoughtfully. "And how will the preachers and deacons be chosen for the new church?" Her whole life, she had belonged to the same district she had been born into, so she didn't know how it was done.

"The new congregation's baptized men and women will nominate whoever they feel is being called as a leader. Any man who receives three votes or more is placed in a pool. The two new preachers will be chosen from the pool."

"That means it could be anyone?" she asked, enjoying the feel of her husband's hand in hers.

"Any man who's been baptized, is married and is in good standing in the church, *ya*."

"But how do you know you've chosen the right men?" she asked.

He looked down at her. "God chooses through us. God always chooses well."

"And you truly believe that?" she asked, appreciating what a man of faith her husband was.

He thought over her question for a moment and looked at her. "I do."

The sound of hoofbeats reverberated on the pavement, and they both looked over their shoulders to see an open wagon headed in the same direction they were going. As the wagon moved closer, Eve realized it was Eli and Ginger. Eli was easy to spot from a distance because of his bright red hair. Ginger, her first pregnancy now obvious to everyone, waved, and Eve waved back.

Then she realized she was still holding Levi's hand and she tried to pull away.

"Ne," Levi told her, holding on. "A man has a right to his wife's hand."

"But it's the Sabbath," she whispered as his sister and her family grew closer.

"The Sabbath is a gift from God, and so is a wife," he told her.

Eli slowed the wagon and called out to them with a grin. "I'd offer you a ride to Ethan and Abigail's, but my wife says I'm to let the newlyweds be."

Levi smiled as they rolled by. "A wise woman, your wife."

Eli glanced at Ginger and called back to them good-naturedly, "Don't I know it."

As they drove away, Eve studied their four little ones in the back of the wagon, all clean and neatly dressed for church, and she couldn't help wondering if some-day she and Levi would be driving to church with their own children. Was it too much to hope for?

She felt the warmth of Levi's hand and prayed it wasn't.

Chapter Ten

Excited to be going on another date with her husband, Eve walked out of the house on a Saturday morning, smoothing the fresh apron she wore over her new blue dress. The fabric Levi had ordered by mail, both sturdy and easy to wash and hang on the line, was perfect for an everyday dress. And it was so beautiful. She had a feeling Rosemary had picked out the fabric because Levi knew nothing about women's clothing, but it didn't matter because it had been his idea that she should have another blue dress.

Eve was so excited for the morning's adventure. Levi was taking her over to Seven Poplars to see Albert Hartman's alpacas. There, she'd also get to meet Rosemary's friend Hannah, whom she'd heard so much about. And after visiting with the Hartmans, they were going to stop at Gideon Esch's shop on the way home to pick up fresh sausage and scrapple.

As Eve followed the oyster shell lane toward the harness shop where she would meet Levi, Jacob's dogs rushed past her. The Chesapeake Bay retrievers crisscrossed in front of her, nipping at each other playfully. She smiled at their antics as they cut behind her and raced toward the house again.

It was going to be another hot August day, with barely a breeze, but the heat wasn't going to bother Eve. She'd cross a desert in a buggy just to sit beside Levi and hear him talk about disc versus drum brakes and the newfangled shocks he wanted to add to his buggy design. She didn't even know what shocks were, but she didn't care. She just liked to hear the sound of Levi's voice.

As she grew closer to the harness shop, her gaze settled on Levi and his father standing in the parking area. There were two buggies and an old blue pickup in the lot, and a white car was coming up the lane. Saturdays were so busy at the shop that Tara was going to be working the cash register every Saturday morning for the foreseeable future.

Eve slowed her pace to study the two men who were obviously father and son. Levi's head was bowed slightly, and Benjamin was staring out in the direction of the hay feed that ran along the side of the oyster shell lane. She didn't have to be there to know that it was another tense conversation between father and son.

She sighed, her heart going out to her husband. She wished there was something she could do to help bridge the gap between the two of them, but Levi had been adamant that it wasn't her concern. He had told her on multiple occasions that his trouble with his father was not her fault, and he had made it plain that he wanted her to stay out of it.

She watched Levi shake his head in disagreement

and wondered what they were discussing. She debated whether she should go to her husband or wait there in the driveway for him. She saw no sign of the buggy they were taking, which meant Levi hadn't made it to the barn yet.

"Eve! Eve!" a voice called from behind.

Eve turned around to see Rosemary hurrying down the lane after her. In her hand was a piece of white paper. Behind her, her and Benjamin's toddlers trailed, both barefoot, and one was carrying a stick. When she'd first arrived, she'd been embarrassed to admit that she couldn't tell the difference between the little boys. However, after James fell off a fence and had to have stitches, it had been easy for her to identify him because of the tiny red scar on his forehead. They were adorable little boys, full of vim and vinegar, as her mother used to say.

"Glad I caught you before you left," Rosemary said, flapping the paper in her hand. She was out of breath by the time she reached Eve. "I completely forgot that Eli asked me yesterday when we'd be picking up an order of scrapple again from Gideon's shop. Would you mind picking up a couple of things for Ginger? Her ankles are swelling up in this heat and the midwife insists she stay off her feet at least a few hours a day." She shook her head as she caught her breath. "Eli's about to come undone. He fusses over her as if he were a mother hen."

Eve smiled, wondering, if God were to bless her and Levi with children someday, if he would be the same. She could imagine how frustrated Ginger probably was with Eli fretting over her, but how good it had to feel to have a husband who cared so much.

"We can do that." Eve accepted the white envelope with the list on the back. Rosemary liked using junk mail to keep her lists. She said envelopes fit nicely in her apron pocket and it was a good way to save on paper. "Levi said he's going to put a cooler in the buggy with some ice."

"Good idea." Rosemary wiped her forehead with the back of her hand. "Going to be another hot one." Her gaze strayed to her little ones, who had wandered off into the grass. They were trying to get one of the dogs to fetch, but so far, it appeared that the dogs were watching the twins play the game.

Eve smiled as she watched James throw the stick and then Josiah run to get it and take it back to his brother. She returned her gaze to Rosemary. "I'm meeting Levi at the harness shop, but—" She exhaled, not sure what to say, so she just looked in that direction.

Rosemary's gaze followed Eve's and settled on the two men in the parking lot. *"Ach,"* she muttered. "Those two, at it again. They're too much alike, I say. They butt heads like two billy goats."

Eve looked at Rosemary. "But it hasn't always been that way, has it? Not before I arrived." The moment the words were out of her mouth, she wished she could take them back. Levi didn't want her talking to his stepmother about him and his father. And her husband certainly didn't want Eve bringing up the suspicious circumstances of their marriage with anyone. Not even in an offhand way.

Rosemary's gaze shifted to Eve and she settled her hands on her hips. In her late forties, she certainly didn't look like she had given birth to eight children in twenty-five years. She was still slender and had barely a gray hair beneath her starched white *kapp*.

"Relationships between a father and son are complicated," Rosemary said. "Especially when the son becomes a man and the father isn't quite ready for that. And sons forget that their fathers aren't always right or fair."

Eve pressed her lips together, running her finger along the edge of the envelope in her hand. It was all she could do not to blurt out how guilty she felt because even though Levi denied it, she knew the trouble between him and his father was all her fault.

Rosemary reached out and stroked Eve's arm. "Both of them are so stubborn. The father thinks he has the right to certain details and the son doesn't. And neither wants to give in."

Eve knew very well Levi's stepmother was referring to their marriage. "And what do you think?" she said softly, not looking at Rosemary.

The older woman sighed. "I think the details Benjamin is seeking no longer matter." She hesitated and then went on. "While I agree that Benjamin had good reason to be concerned when you and Levi arrived in June, it's plain to see you two are finding your stride in your marriage. And I think in time, my husband will see that and let go of whatever anger or disappointment he's still holding on to."

Eve looked up, fighting tears that she could feel working their way out. She didn't know what to say. Her heart was so filled by Rosemary's kindness that she couldn't find the words to thank her.

"Marriage isn't easy, not for anyone," Rosemary went

on. "Benjamin and I hit a couple bumps on the path in our early days before moving here." She smiled, seeming lost in memory. "And I can tell you that Levi's father, my first husband, and I went head-to-head in the beginning. We were so young and headstrong and self-ish sometimes, I think. But, with time, we found our way. Together. As God intended."

Rosemary glanced over to where her boys were playing. They were now using the stick to dig a hole. She returned her attention to Eve. "I guess what I'm trying to say, in a roundabout way, is that I'm not worried about you and Levi anymore. I was at first. I could tell the two of you weren't in harmony. But I see the changes, and my heart is glad for you both. And Benjamin will get there, too. Levi just needs to be patient."

Eve smiled. "I wish you'd tell him that."

Rosemary chuckled. "I tell them both, sometimes at the same time, but—" she shrugged "—men. With matters of the heart, they can move at a snail's pace."

Eve met Rosemary's gaze. *"Danke."*

Rosemary drew back, her green eyes crinkling at the corners. "For what?"

"For your kindness." Eve lowered her head and then raised it again to look her in the eye. "For welcoming me here, even if it wasn't in the circumstances you had expected. I'm so happy here, and part of that is because of you, Rosemary."

The older woman smiled. *"Ach,* I'm glad you're happy." She gestured with her chin in the direction of the harness shop. "Now, what say you and I break up this discussion between our husbands before they raise their voices and scare off all our customers."

Eve laughed at Rosemary's practicality and walked beside her, the list tucked safely in her pocket, along with hope that her relationship with Levi's stepmother would only grow stronger over time.

The following church Sunday, Levi stood a few feet from a group of older men who had gathered beside the Fishers' fence, his hands deep in his pockets, head bowed so that the brim of his wool hat shielded his face. He couldn't hear what was being said, but he didn't need to. He had heard his name spoken, and by the body language he was observing, he knew what they were saying.

After services and the midday meal, those adults who would become a part of the new church district had gathered to accept nominations for the two preacher positions and one deacon. Members of the congregation had been instructed two weeks before to spend time in prayer to seek God's will in their new church's founding. The duties of the preachers would be to give sermons at services. The new deacon would serve as Bishop Simon's assistant of sorts. He would collect donations, when required, in their community, speak to those in need of moral righting or counseling, and make marriage announcements, among other duties. Deacons and preachers were unpaid, and many hours and sacrifices were required from both the candidate and his family. They were no positions any man wanted, but when called by his people, by God, it was a sacrifice required by their faith.

Earlier, folks had stood and called out names. Any man whose name was given up three times or more would be included in the list of possible candidates. At the next church service in two weeks, two slips of paper would be placed in two hymnals, and those books would be placed in a stack with hymnals that did not have a slip of paper in them. Each man whose name has been offered up as a possible preacher would choose a hymnal. The two men who chose the hymnals with the slips of paper in them would be the men God had chosen to be the new preachers. The same process would take place to select a new deacon.

Levi's gaze shifted to his father, who stood in the circle of men. His heart ached that his father still believed he had sinned and not confessed. All men and women sinned; that was a given. But to not to confess—that was what stuck in his father's craw. He knew that because during their evening prayers, led by his father, the subject was often addressed.

Levi had probably been more surprised than anyone else the first time his name was announced as a possible preacher candidate. Having his name repeated twice more had shocked him. So he would be one of the men to choose a hymnal during the next service. And possibly become one of their preachers.

The first time his name was spoken, he'd heard a shuffle of feet, a few whispers. By the third time, there were audible sounds. No one spoke, but throats were cleared, and there was coughing and shifting on the pews.

It was obvious to Levi that there were those who did not believe his name should be in the pool. Because Levi had married without his parents' knowledge, everyone had jumped to the conclusion that he had sinned. Because they believed that Levi was not a man right with God and should not, therefore, be considered.

Levi stood there a few minutes longer, listening to the rumble of the men's voices. A raindrop fell on his hand and he looked up into the sky. The air was humid and rainclouds were gathering.

He wondered if he ought to find Eve and set off for home. If they didn't go soon, they'd get wet on the two-mile walk, but it was either walk or get into a buggy with his father, and right now, he didn't know if he could do that.

Just as Levi was about to turn away, he heard his father's strong baritone voice. "I value everyone's thoughts on this matter, but I have to ask you this…" He paused, looking from one man to the next, taking his time, drawing their undivided attention. "Do we trust in the process?"

"What?" someone asked.

"Do we believe in this process of selection for our church?" Levi's father asked.

Men responded one after another.

"Ya."

"We do."

"It's how it's done. How it's always been done," came the voices.

"Then why, my friends," he asked, "would we remove a man's name that has been offered up not once, but three times by our congregation?" Again, Levi's father paused. He waited for a ripple of muted utterances to pass and then went on. "If we trust this process, if we accept that it is God who will be choosing these men by setting their hand on the right hymnal, why would we think we should remove a name from the candidates?"

No one said anything. Men stared at their shoes.

"If Levi Miller is not meant to be a preacher, God will not choose him," his father said in a calm, steady voice.

Sadness washed over Levi. His father had not defended him, only the process. His father didn't think him fit to be a preacher.

Levi walked away.

He crossed the barnyard as the sky grew darker and walked up to the house. Spotting his brother Jesse, he called out to him. "Have you seen Eve?"

Jesse was sitting on the porch rail with two boys about the same age. "*Ya*, in the kitchen, I think."

"Could you go inside and tell her I'm ready to go?"

Thirteen-year-old Jesse, who had grown tall and lanky over the summer, jumped down from the rail. "But Levi. It's going to rain. That's why—"

"Please do as I ask," Levi interrupted.

Without another word, Jesse went into the house.

Levi walked out to Marshall's driveway and waited. A few minutes later, Eve hurried down the porch steps, her bonnet in her hand.

"What's wrong?" she asked as she joined him.

"It's going to rain. If we don't go now, we'll get wet." Levi started down the driveway toward the road.

Eve put her bonnet on her head and began to tie it under her chin. "That's why we brought two buggies, so—"

"I'm going home. Come with me," he intoned,

lengthening his stride. "Or stay and return with my family. Your choice."

She hurried to catch up with him, hurt obvious in her voice. "*You* are my family, Levi. Of course I'll come home with you."

They walked in silence to the road and turned toward home before she spoke again. "What's wrong?" she asked.

He kept walking. He wanted to tell her, but he was afraid he would cry if he spoke of it right now. He knew his father was disappointed in him, but he couldn't believe he hadn't spoken up for his own son's character.

"Levi, please," Eve murmured, slipping her arm through his. "Please talk to me."

He shook his head. "Not now," he muttered.

And then the rain began in earnest and he wondered if it had been a mistake ever coming home to Hickory Grove.

On her hands and knees, Eve spread the thick green leaves of the closest sprawling plant and spied a cucumber just the right size and color for picking. She snapped it off the vine and added it to the peck basket in the row between her and Tara.

"You're quiet today," Tara said. "What's troubling you?"

Eve took a moment to respond. A part of her thought she shouldn't say anything about Levi. He was her husband and it wasn't right to talk about him behind his back. But a part of her thought it was time she did something. Else she feared their marriage might not ever be what she had begun to think was possible.

Eve had tried to be patient with Levi. For two full days, she had kept quiet and waited for him to tell her why he had become so upset after church on Sunday. She had waited for him to tell her why he had barely spoken to her, to anyone since leaving Lovey and Marshall's. She suspected it had something to do with his name being one of the five who had been proposed for preacher, but she had no way of knowing because he wouldn't tell her.

That morning, now the third day, she had stood in the doorway of their bedroom, blocking his escape, and asked him outright what had him so upset. She didn't tell him that his black mood made her fear they were losing everything they had accomplished in their marriage in the last two months. Since church on Sunday, he had gone back to avoiding her, barely speaking, and bordered on rudeness with her and his family. He had turned so far inward that she wasn't only worried about the health of their marriage, but about him.

Levi had refused to meet her gaze. He told her he would talk about it when he was ready and he wasn't ready. And then he had ducked under her arm and walked out of their bedroom.

Eve had been so frustrated, so angry with him, that she had wanted to throw something at him. Not something hard that would hurt him—maybe a pillow or a balled-up sock, something to knock some sense into him.

"Did I do something wrong?" Tara asked, getting Eve's attention again.

Eve sat up, settling her dusty hands in her lap. She was quiet for a moment and then made a decision. "It's

Levi," she said softly. "He's not been himself since church Sunday and I'm not sure why."

Tara looked surprised. "He didn't tell you?"

"Tell me what?"

Tara, who'd been picking cucumbers a few feet ahead of Eve, crawled the distance between them and sat up. Her knees pressed against Eve's. "There was a big hullabaloo after services," she said in a half whisper.

Eve frowned, feeling her forehead crease. "About what?"

"Choosing the preachers!" She leaned closer. "Some people don't think Levi is an acceptable candidate."

"Why?" Eve asked, slapping at a mosquito. Since the rain Sunday, they had been bad. Because of the pests, she and Tara had waited until late morning when the sun was higher, but not so high as to be roasting, to come out to pick cucumbers to make pickles.

Tara bit down on her lower lip.

Eve rose to her knees and grabbed Tara's hand. "Please, Tara. You have to tell me because Levi won't… or can't. And I can't help him if I don't know what's wrong."

Tara pursed her lips. "*Mam* says I need to do a better job of minding my own knitting."

Eve released her. "This is not gossip. I'm Levi's wife, and I need to help him. And I need your help to do that." She frowned. "Why don't they think Levi should be considered for the job of preacher?"

Tara folded her hands in her lap and looked down at them. Her cheeks reddened. "Because no one knew you were getting married," she whispered under her breath.

"And... And some say he should have made a confession to Bishop Simon."

Tara's words practically knocked the wind out of Eve, and she sat back hard on her heels.

"I'm sorry," Tara said softly. "That's what Martha Gruber said she heard her mother telling their neighbor."

Wiping her damp brow, Eve looked away. The huge garden was beautiful, with its neat rows of bright green plants and the soft, turned-up soil that created paths between them. She watched a butterfly flutter above a flower in a small patch of mixed wildflowers. Rosemary had interspersed beds of herbs as well as flowers in the vegetable garden.

Eve took a breath and turned back to Tara. "It's okay," she assured her. "It's going to be all right." She straightened her spine. "Levi and I are going to figure this out." She glanced across the garden to stare at the big dairy barn in the distance. Then she looked back at Tara. "Could you finish up picking the cucumbers? I have something I have to do."

"*Ya*, of course, *Schweschder*." Tara offered a shy smile. "I would do anything for you."

Touched that Tara would call her sister, Eve threw her arms around the younger girl and hugged her tightly. Determined to get to the bottom of this matter with her husband, she rose, dusted bits of dirt and leaves off her apron and strode barefoot down the row.

She was scared, but she would go to Levi. Because she wanted their marriage to be a good one. And even though he didn't love her, she was still hopeful that someday he would.

Chapter Eleven

At first, Eve was disappointed when she didn't find Levi in his shop. Then she was annoyed when Bay, who was busy watering mums in her greenhouse, told Eve that he had left in a wagon an hour previously to repair a buggy axle a good distance away. When Eve had asked her how long she thought he'd been gone, she'd shrugged and said something about as grumpy as he'd been, she was hoping he'd be gone a week or so.

With nothing to do but wait, Eve went about her day. She returned to the garden to help Tara finish harvesting cucumbers and then spent hours washing them, slicing them, and making bread and butter pickles to can. Again and again, she went to the kitchen window, hoping to see the wagon parked near the shop. As the hours on the wall clock ticked by, she went from being annoyed with her husband to becoming worried. He'd never said a word to her about being gone all day, and she began to fear that he'd been in an accident on the road. It wasn't unheard of. Horse and buggies and wagons were hit on the road all the time, and Amish folks died in those kinds of accidents.

When Levi finally walked into the house, Eve was putting supper on the table. Her chest heaving with relief, she had greeted him with a smile, but he only nodded and excused himself to wash up.

Levi was quiet through the entire meal of cold ham slices, chow-chow, mustard potato salad and sweet and sour beets. He didn't even comment on the cheddar biscuits he had to know she'd made fresh just for him. Several times as the evening dragged, Eve tried to make eye contact with him, hoping they could step outside together to talk, but he avoided her gaze.

After evening prayers, Eve climbed the stairs alone, prepared for bed and waited for her husband in their bedroom. He was so long in coming that she feared he wasn't, but she was still awake when he opened the door.

Levi walked into their bedroom and seemed startled to find her sitting on the edge of the bed. She'd washed up and was wearing a white summer nightgown Rosemary had given her. Eve's prayer *kapp* was lying neatly on top of the chest of drawers, stuffed with white paper to keep its shape. She wore her hair loose down her back, which fell to her waist.

He looked so surprised that, for a moment, she feared he might turn around and walk out.

"Close the door," she said softly, but in a tone that told him she meant business.

He hovered in the doorway. "Eve—"

"Close the door," she repeated evenly, making a point

to keep her voice down. "Unless you want everyone in this house to hear what I have to say."

He got a stricken look on his face and closed the door.

Eve pressed her lips together. She'd been rehearsing what she wanted to say to him, but now her knees were shaking beneath her gown. She sent a little prayer heavenward, asking for God's help in finding the words she needed to get through to her husband. Her whole life, she'd tried to be quiet, meek and mild. She had tried to be the woman her father wanted her to be. He had warned her repeatedly that it was not a woman's place to speak against a man. She imagined he had given her mother the same lecture.

But what if her mother had spoken up when her father had tried to silence her? Would her father have become a different man? If Eve's mother had established a different sort of marriage in their early days as husband and wife, would her father have not grown to be so harsh and rigid?

On Sunday, the deacon had read a verse from the Bible that came to Eve's mind. The only words she could recall right now were: *Be courageous, be strong.* Had those words been meant for her? For this moment?

When she heard the sound of the door click closed, she stood up. "Why didn't you tell me?" she asked.

He pressed a thumb and forefinger to his temples and blinked. He looked tired. "Tell you what?"

"That people spoke up against you after church. That there are those who—" Her words got caught in her throat and she had to take a moment before she could go on. "There are those who think you aren't fit to be a preacher."

His hand fell to his side and his gaze to his bare feet. He'd already cleaned up for bed. "I didn't want to be a preacher anyway."

She took a step toward him. "That's not the point, Levi. It's not up to you. It's up to *Gott*," she said, somehow finding the strength she needed to keep from backing down. To say what needed to be said.

He set his jaw, still not meeting her gaze.

"You should have told me," she repeated. "I'm your wife, and to make this marriage work, we have to be able to tell each other things. Even if we're embarrassed. Even if they hurt."

"I'm sorry," he murmured, shaking his head. "It was only that I didn't want to...upset you."

"Not a good reason." She crossed her arms over her chest. "Those people who spoke against you, it's because of me, isn't it? It's because we married so quickly and everyone made the assumption that we—" She felt her cheeks grow warm with embarrassment, but she pressed on because this was not the time to be shy and girlish. "They thought we acted as man and wife when we were not." She hesitated and then asked, "Is that why you're so upset? Because they don't think you are morally fit to speak God's word?"

He sighed and pressed his hand to his forehead. "*Ne*, I don't care about what others think. God knows what I have or have not done. But—" His voice cracked. "I... I overheard the men talking about it after services. My father was among them and he spoke up."

"For you?"

"*Ne*, wife. Not for me. For the tradition. For the way we choose our preachers and deacons. He said that they should trust in the process because God would not choose me because of my sin."

Eve's breath caught and it took her a moment to find her voice. "Oh, Levi," she murmured. She glanced at the window that reflected the light from the oil lamp beside the bed. She looked back at him. "This is all because of me. Because I disobeyed my father and got myself into trouble."

He lifted his hand in a tired gesture. "See, that's why I didn't tell you. Because you'd say it was your fault."

"Because it is!" she responded in frustration. "I made a terrible mistake with terrible costs, and you offered to marry me to protect me. You saved me, Levi."

He lowered his gaze to the floor again.

She sighed. "You have to tell him," she said, her voice calm again. "You have to tell your father and Rosemary what happened to me. Why you married me. And you have to tell our bishop, too. He'll know what to do about the gossip."

"*Ne, ne*, Eve." Levi shook his head again and again. "I told you I would never speak to anyone of how we came to be husband and wife. I will not speak a word of this to our bishop. As to my father, if he doesn't know me better than this, then—" He exhaled sharply. *"Ne,"* he repeated again. "I will not do it." Then he reached around her and grabbed the pillow, blanket and sheet he'd been using for his pallet on the floor from the end of the bed.

Before Eve could protest, he was out the door, closing it behind him.

Eve brought her hands to her face, near to bursting into tears. Instead, she took a couple of deep breaths and lowered herself to her knees. Clasping her hands together, she rested her elbows on the bed, squeezed her eyes shut and prayed fervently to God. Because if she didn't do something, she feared the marriage she thought could be possible would never come to be.

"Dear *Gott*, what do I do?" she whispered. "How do I make this right for my husband? How do I save my marriage?"

And God's response came to her as loud and clear in her head as if He had been in the room.

Levi did not return to their bedroom, but Eve slept surprisingly well that night. In the morning, she rose before anyone else in the family, just as the sun was washing the day in all of its glory. Wearing her favorite blue dress, her hair tucked neatly in a bun under her *kapp*, she went down to the kitchen and put two large percolators of coffee on the gas stove. When it was ready, she poured a cup black, the way Levi liked it, and went in search of him.

Eve located her husband in a tiny bedroom on the second floor that was used for storage. When she pushed open the door, she found him asleep in his clothes, curled up on some old sleeping bags on the floor.

"Levi?" she whispered. When he didn't respond, she leaned over and touched his shoulder gently. "Levi, wake up. It's morning."

He rolled over onto his back and opened his eyes. He looked at her, then the single window where sunlight poured in, then at her again.

"Best you get up before anyone else finds you here," she said. Then she set his cup of coffee beside him on the floor and walked out of the room before he had a chance to respond.

By the time Tara arrived downstairs, Eve had three baking sheets of bacon in the oven and was mixing up ingredients for blueberry muffins. Lovey had sent an entire bucket of blueberries over the day before, and while most would be frozen for use later, there was nothing better than fresh blueberries in a muffin.

"You're up early," Tara said, going to the dish cabinet to begin setting the table. "Are you all right?"

Standing at the kitchen counter, Eve took a deep breath. *Was* she all right?

She was.

Because her prayer had been answered. Because she knew what she had to do. And she knew it was the right thing.

"*Ya*, I'm *goot*." Eve smiled at Tara and shrugged. "I woke early, so I thought I'd get a start on breakfast."

"Sorry I slept in," Tara said. Then she whispered, "I was up late reading a book Chloe gave me. It's a *romance*." She grinned.

Eve cut her eyes at Tara but said nothing. Whether Tara's parents would approve of her reading choice wasn't her concern. At least it wasn't today. As her mother had always said, she had bigger fish to fry.

Eve returned to the task at hand, adding baking powder to the dry ingredients. Once the flour, salt and leavening were properly mixed, she would fold in the wet ingredients. She would mix it just until the flour and such were wet, paying no attention to a few lumps. Then she would add the blueberries, continuing to gently stir so as not to make the muffins tough. Once they were in greased tins, they would have fresh blueberry muffins in half an hour.

Levi managed to arrive at the breakfast table just in time for the silent prayer of thanks. He sat beside Eve the entire meal, not looking at her or anyone else. If anybody noticed, they didn't speak up.

The family laughed and teased as they ate, often talking over one another. Eve tried to keep up with every conversation, but as usual, it was near impossible. Bay went on about a new type of poinsettia plant that was growing well in the greenhouse. Benjamin complained about the cost of shipping for items he had to order for the harness shop, and Jesse told a long story about a goat that seemed to go nowhere and arrived at no conclusion. James and Josiah managed to each spill their milk not once, but twice over the course of the meal. It was a typical breakfast.

Levi spoke to Eve a couple of times during the meal, and not unkindly. She could tell he was upset with himself about their disagreement the night before, but he didn't say anything more than to ask her to pass the butter or another blueberry muffin. When everyone scattered after breakfast, Levi lingered in the mudroom, fussing with his hat. It seemed as if he wanted to speak with Eve privately, but she gave him no mind. She knew she had to take matters into her own hands, and that was what she intended to do.

When everyone had set off on their day's business, including Levi, who would be working in his shop today, Eve helped Tara clean up. Tara chattered as they went about their familiar tasks, talking about plans to go with her friend Chloe to pick sunflowers in a neighbor's field that afternoon.

When the kitchen was at last *ret* up, Eve hung the damp dish towels on the handles of the stove and asked Tara, "Do you know where your *mam* is?"

Tara was moving food around in the open refrigerator, taking stock to be sure everything was on the grocery list for shopping the following day. "In her sewing room, I think. James tore the knees out of another pair of pants." She rolled her eyes.

Eve chuckled and walked out of the kitchen. She followed a long hallway to the open door of Rosemary's sewing room. She heard the steady sound of a treadle sewing machine coming from inside, and she took a deep breath. If she was going to do this, now was the time. She took a deep breath, said a silent prayer and knocked on the doorframe. "Rosemary?"

The sound of the sewing machine paused. "*Ya!* Come in."

Eve walked into the room to see Rosemary seated at her Singer sewing machine. The sound began again as Levi's stepmother used both feet to pump the treadle and eased the seam of a small pair of navy trousers through the needle.

"Almost done. Just two more seams," Rosemary said above the *click, click* sound measured out by the rhythm of her feet.

"No hurry," Eve answered, gazing around. Rosemary had invited her to use the sewing machine anytime and, on several occasions, she'd spent a comfortable afternoon here. Besides the blue dress she had made, she'd also sewn herself a second nightgown and a pale green work shirt for Levi. She was presently working on a black wool coat for her husband to wear to church when it grew colder. The one currently hanging on a hook in their bedroom was threadbare at the cuffs and missing a hook and eye, and he had admitted sheepishly that he had been wearing it since before his family moved to Hickory Grove.

Nearly square, the sewing room was painted a pale blue with two large windows with a blue, white and yellow rag rug in the middle of the floor. There were two rocking chairs placed side by side where sisters, or mother and daughter, or mother-in-law and daughter-in-law, could sit and knit. One wall boasted an oversize walnut cabinet that looked like it had come from an old millinery shop. Eve recognized the style from one she had seen displayed in a Lancaster fabric store once. Open drawers in Rosemary's cabinet revealed various sizes of thread, needles, scissors and paper patterns. A small knotty pine table with turned legs stood between the windows, and in its center was a big terracotta planter filled with flowers.

Tara had told Eve that her mother changed the flowers with the seasons. While there were multicolored zinnias blooming in it now, this fall, there would be white or gold chrysanthemums. In December, Rosemary would replace the mums with poinsettias, and after Epiphany, it would be filled with herbs like rosemary and tarragon to be used in winter soups and stews. When Tara had told Eve this, she had giggled. Her mother's naming of her daughters had been unusual for an Amish woman, she had admitted. And then she had gone on to explain. Tara was named after the herb tarragon. Her sister Nettie's name was actually Nettle, Bay's was Bay Laurel and her oldest sister, Lovey, was Lovage.

"Ach," Rosemary cried as she ceased pumping the treadle. "One seam left to go, and the thread breaks in the needle." She raised her hands as if in surrender. "Always happens, doesn't it?" She turned on the bench where she sat to look at Eve and fell silent for a moment. "What's troubling you, Eve? I can see it on your face."

Eve clasped her hands and looked down at her clean, bare feet. Suddenly, she was unsure of herself. Was this a mistake to come to Rosemary? Was it wrong to go against her husband's wishes? The husband was the head of the family. Some believed that as his wife, she was required to obey him.

"Let me guess. This has something to do with that dejected look on Levi's face that we saw at the breakfast table." Rosemary got to her feet. "And my stubborn husband."

Eve slowly lifted her gaze, steeling herself so that she wouldn't cry. *"Ya."*

"Then tell me, but first, I think you need a hug. Then you should sit down and unburden yourself." Rosemary smiled kindly. "I can't tell you how pleased I am that you feel you can come to me, Eve."

Eve's voice trembled a little when she spoke. "Levi wouldn't like it if he knew I was here. He… He thinks this is between him and Benjamin."

"Ya." Rosemary planted her hands on her hips. "But we've left it up to those two for the hind part of two months, haven't we? And have they settled it? They have

not. So it's time we women had a hand it." She opened her arms. "Come on. Let me give you a hug, *Dochter*. You look as if you need it."

Eve hesitated, then stepped closer and allowed Rosemary to hug her. "This is all my fault," she told Rosemary, fighting against tears again. Her mother-in-law's arms felt good around her and she hugged her back. "Levi is such a good man and I've ruined his life."

Rosemary clasped Eve's shoulders and leaned back to look into her eyes. "*Ne*, you have made his life. And life has its hills and valleys. Now come and sit with me and tell me what's weighing on your heart. Because I have to tell you, I've about had enough of this quarrel with these men of ours. They're bringing disharmony to our home and heartburn to Benjamin's stomach."

Rosemary smiled with amusement and Eve couldn't help but smile back.

So she and Rosemary sat side by side and Eve told her story. She started with the charming Jemuel Yoder at the market and barely took a breath until she finished with her and Levi's wedding day. Throughout the story, Rosemary listened patiently, asking questions occasionally and patting Eve's knee when her voice trembled.

When she was done, Eve took a deep breath and slid farther into the rocking chair. She was so short that only her toes touched the floor when she sat all the way back.

"Oh, my poor dear," Rosemary said when Eve fell silent. "I'm so sad about everything you've been through." She reached out and squeezed Eve's hand. "And thankful that God brought you to us. You're truly a blessing to this family."

Eve took a shuddering breath. "I don't think Levi feels that way right now."

"And why do you say that?" Rosemary asked pointedly. "Has Levi said that to you?"

Eve thought before she answered. "He has not. He… He promised to protect my secret. He said he would never tell anyone about Jemuel. About my father."

Rosemary smiled kindly. "That's our Levi. A kind, admirable man. A good man."

"He is a good man," Eve said, twisting a bit of her apron between her fingers. "I don't deserve him."

"Nonsense," Rosemary responded. "Do you love him?" Her question was pointed. "Or at least do you think you can love him in time? I'm not talking about the girlish, giggling kind of love. I'm talking about the deep love that binds us all of our days."

"He doesn't love me."

Rosemary gave a little laugh. "I suspect he does. Whether he knows it or not, that's why this has been so hard for him. That's why he can't ask you to let him tell his father why you married." She took Eve's hand. "And you didn't answer my question. *Do you love Levi?*"

The warmth of Rosemary's hand gave Eve the strength to respond with honesty. "I do love him. And that's why I have to make this right." She went on faster. "I can't stand having his father think he committed a sin he didn't commit. Nor his community. And I can't have our bishop and our congregation believing that, either," she added firmly.

Both women were silent for a moment. Then Eve said, "I want to talk to Bishop Simon. I want to tell him everything. Will you take me?"

Rosemary squeezed Eve's hand and got up from her rocking chair. She paced one way across the sewing room and then the other. "Are you certain about this?" she asked. "You have the right—you and Levi have the right—to keep this to yourselves."

Eve set her jaw. "I'm certain."

"And are you certain this isn't because you want Levi to be a preacher? Some women, especially young women, think it makes them more important in the community. To have a husband who serves as preacher or deacon."

Eve drew back in horror. "Why would I want my husband to spend long hours away from me, planning his sermons, making visits with the bishop and deacon, always having the responsibility of the church on his shoulders? I don't know if Levi is supposed to be a preacher." She got to her feet. "That's up to God. But I want Bishop Simon to know that Levi Miller is a Godly man. And I want Benjamin to know the truth about his son."

Rosemary came to a rest in front of Eve. "And you've really thought this through?" she asked, looking into Eve's eyes.

"*Ya.* I've thought for weeks that it was the right thing to do, and then when Levi's name came up at church, I knew…" She glanced away and then back to Rosemary. "I prayed on it and God answered me," she said, half-afraid Rosemary wouldn't believe her. Who was she, a plain little wren of a woman, to hear God's voice?

Rosemary took a deep breath. "Well, I suppose a trip to Bishop Simon's place is in order," she declared, walking to the sewing room door.

Eve felt a moment of panic. "What? Now?"

"*Ya*, now. No time like the present, and if we go now, we can still be back in time to get dinner on the table."

And so they did. Eve was surprised how easy Bishop Simon was to talk to. Over a glass of lemonade on his front porch, in Rosemary's presence, she spilled out the whole story, and with it her tears of regret as well as hope.

The bishop thanked Eve for coming to him and told her again and again what a fine wife she was and what a good life God had in store for her and Levi. Then he instructed her to say nothing to Levi or Benjamin. To leave the matter to him. He told Eve and Rosemary that he needed to pray on the matter and that he would be by their farm in the next couple of days.

So Eve waited, busying herself with canning tomatoes and beets and making pickles with Tara, and trying not to dream of a life with Levi and a houseful of little ones.

Chapter Twelve

Levi was giving a piece of trim work for the dashboard a final sanding when, from the window in his shop, he spotted the bishop's buggy pulling in. His first thought, childishly, was to slip into the warren of halls and rooms his father had constructed in the old barn and hide until Bishop Simon gave up looking for him and went home.

But even if he avoided Simon today, Levi couldn't hide from him forever. And he couldn't hide from the decision he had made when he offered to marry Eve and promised to never tell anyone why. So if the bishop asked Levi his side of the story, Levi would tell him nothing. He would not sacrifice his vow to his wife, not even to defend his own morality. And that would be that. The bishop would say Levi left him no choice but to remove his name from the list of preacher candidates. And that would be that.

Levi didn't really want to be a preacher anyway. It was a lot of work that took a man away from family and work, often causing financial consequences. And being a preacher, responsible for speaking God's word to His people, was a heavy burden on a man's soul. Levi didn't feel he had a calling to stand up in front of a congregation and preach God's word. He had been as surprised as anyone when his name had come up, not once but three times.

Of course, had this whole mess unraveled differently and he was a candidate, and he did choose the hymnal with the slip of paper, he would not have turned down the position. It would have been his duty to his congregation and to God. Because when God called a man to be a preacher, the man responded with faith that his Lord would give him the words to speak.

But all of that was a moot point now, Levi thought with a tired sigh. With time, the whole thing would blow over and few would even remember who could have been a preacher but wasn't chosen. But Levi would remember. He would recall that members of his tight-knit community had deemed him unfit for the role. And his father could be counted among them.

With resignation, Levi flipped over the board he was sanding and ran his finger along the edge, feeling for any burrs. At least the construction of his very first buggy was going well. That was something, wasn't it?

"Levi," Bishop Simon called as he walked into the buggy shop. He was wearing black pants, a white shirt, black vest and his wide-brimmed black hat—this was an official call.

Levi glanced up and acknowledged the older man with a nod.

The bishop was a short, round man with perpetually rosy cheeks and frameless eyeglasses that he wore on the tip of his bulbous nose. When Levi had first met

Bishop Simon, he had wondered how the glasses didn't slip off his nose and fall on the ground.

Levi liked the older man. He was kind and jovial, a good man who took the responsibility of looking after his flock seriously.

His hands deep in his pockets, Bishop Simon studied the new buggy frame Levi had resting up off the floor on wood chocks. "Going to be a fine-looking carriage," he mused. "I've been told you're a gifted craftsman, Levi. And the telling was accurate." He took a step closer to the shell and peered down over the top of his glasses. "Annie and I have been talking about getting a new buggy. I'm still driving the one my father drove before me. Body has been patched more times than I can tell you, front axle keeps bending, and the windshield is leaking again."

"I can have a look at the windshield. I might be able to pop it out and then put it back in with a new seal and caulk it. Axles can be replaced. If you just want to fix it," Levi told him. "If it's a new buggy you're looking for, I'm taking orders. This one is for my brother-in-law Eli. He and Ginger are in need of a bigger buggy."

Bishop Simon nodded approvingly. "I'll discuss it with Annie. I'm thinking a new one might be in order." He slid his hands from his pockets as he turned to look at Levi. "Do you have time to talk to me for a few minutes, Levi?"

Feeling his shoulders slump, Levi set down his sanding block. *"Ya,"* he said dejectedly. "I've time." He wondered how he would tell Eve his name had been withdrawn because their congregation and their bishop thought him unfit. It wasn't a thing a man wanted to have to admit to his wife. And in his case, it would lead to another discussion with her insisting he had to tell the bishop why he had married her.

Bishop Simon faced Levi. "I'm going to come right out and say this."

Levi heard a strange buzzing in his head, and he glanced away, trying to emotionally steady himself.

"I know everything," Bishop Simon said.

Levi blinked, looking back at the older man in confusion. "Everything about what?"

"About Eve. About why you married her. Why there was no formal betrothal before the wedding."

It took a moment for Levi to process the bishop's words. Surely he had misheard. But the way Simon was considering him, it didn't seem that he had. Because Simon didn't look disappointed, he looked...*pleased*.

"I'm sorry?" Levi narrowed his gaze. "*How* do you know?"

"Eve told me. Yesterday."

Levi's eyes widened in shock. "She came to you?"

"She did. She and Rosemary. Your wife came because of what some people in our congregation have been saying," the bishop explained. "It was important to Eve that I know that you marrying her, without following our usual traditions, was for honorable reasons."

Levi stared at the bishop, still not quite believing what he was hearing. "Eve told you?" he repeated.

Bishop Simon nodded, the slightest smile turning up one corner of his mouth. "She told me the whole story, start to finish. I was sorely sorry to hear how her father treated her." The white cat, Snowball, curled around his leg and he leaned over to stroke her soft coat. "She made a mistake in not listening to her father when he warned her about such men, even among our own. But young folks make mistakes." His smile broadened. "As do old folks. Which brings me to the apology I owe you."

Levi had no idea what to say. What reason could a bishop have to apologize to him?

Simon cleared his throat, looking up at Levi through the smudged lenses of his glasses. "I have to admit that I kept expecting you to show up at my house to talk over whatever brought you and Eve to this place in your lives. I anticipated a confession and forgiveness for your and Eve's sins. Only as time passed, and you didn't come to me, did I begin to suspect there was more to the story than at first glance."

"I can't believe she told you," Levi murmured, a strange sensation in his chest. He pressed his hand to his beating heart. *For him.* Eve had done this for *him.* She had confessed her own missteps to the bishop for Levi's sake.

"She didn't have to tell you," Levi heard himself say. "I would never have asked her to do that for me."

"*Ne,* she did not have to tell me. She explained that. She said that you had promised her no one would ever have to know. And I believe that you would never have told, Levi. Which is why she came to me on her own. It was important to her that I know the truth about you. To know you did not act inappropriately. She wanted me to know that you should be eligible for the position of preacher."

"But I told her I didn't want to be a preacher anyway."

"I don't think Eve thought it mattered what you want.

She believes it should be left to God. And I agree."
Bishop Simon stroked his beard. "That said, Eve told
me, should you be chosen, you would make a fine
preacher. She talked to me about what a man of faith
you are. How your quiet faith has made hers stronger."

"Quiet faith?" Levi asked. He was completely overwhelmed by the sacrifice Eve had made for him. And
her confidence in him. He was so astounded, in fact,
that he was struggling to follow the conversation.

"Eve says you live your faith every day in deed as
much as word and that you set a good example for her.
She said you were there for her, a stranger, when her
own family wasn't willing to stand up for her."

Levi smiled, not because his wife had praised him to
the bishop, but because she thought those things of him.
"She's a good woman. Better than I deserve."

"I think you deserve each other. Talking to Eve, and
knowing you as I do, I believe this was God's plan.
Bringing you together." He tilted his head. "An unusual
way to bring a man and woman together in matrimony,
I'd admit. But as Paul said in his letter to the Romans,
'And we know that all things work together for good
to them that love God, to them who are called according to his purpose.'"

Levi, actually feeling a little light-headed, sat down on
a stool his father used when tackling a time-consuming
task. His head was spinning. Suddenly, all he could think
of was that he needed to talk to Eve.

Simon stroked his long, gray beard. "I have to say,
Levi, I was uneasy when others expressed concern over
your eligibility to be a preacher. Not so much because
I was worried about you, but because unrest of this

sort is not good for our community. I didn't know why
you had married so swiftly, but as I said, I suspected
you had good reason. I told your father that when he
came to me."

Levi looked up. "*Dat* came to you about me?"

"*Ya*, more than once. I counseled that he be patient,
and we prayed together. We discussed the idea that
he needed to believe in you and have faith in God. I
told him all would be revealed in time. If it was God's
will." He raised his hands and let them fall. "And all
has been revealed. So I will not be withdrawing your
name. Should you, when the time comes, choose the
hymnal with a slip of paper in it, you will be one of
my preachers. And your wife is right, I think. A fine
preacher you'll make."

Feeling a little steadier, Levi got up from his father's stool. "I don't know. Maybe I should just let you
withdraw my name, Bishop. I don't want anyone in the
congregation to know about Eve's past. It's not their
business. I don't mind that you know what happened
to Eve because she told you, but I don't want others to
know and possibly judge her. I see no need."

The bishop chewed on that thought for a moment.
"I agree, Levi. It's not necessary that the other parish-
ioners know the circumstances. I've prayed heavily on
this matter and come to the conclusion that it's not my
place to interfere in God's ways. I will not be withdrawing your name. Your name was offered up, so you must
be one of the men to choose a hymnal."

Levi ran his hand over his short beard, still not used
to feeling it. "But what will you say to anyone who questions my suitability? Some folks are going to want an

explanation. Details." Eunice Gruber immediately came to mind, but he didn't say it.

"They won't be getting details from me. I'll tell the congregation I know why you and Eve married and that I have deemed you a suitable candidate. That will be the end of the discussion."

A knock on the inner door that led deeper into the barn sounded and both men turned around to face it. *"Ya?"* Levi called, wondering who was knocking on the shop door from the inside. Any potential customers would be approaching from the outside entrance.

The door swung open and his father filled the doorway. *"Oll recht* if I come in now?" he asked.

"Now?" Levi asked, looking to Bishop Simon.

"I told your father what happened to Eve," the bishop admitted.

"Don't be angry with him," Levi's father said, crossing the shop to join them. "I went to Simon yesterday, not knowing Eve and Rosemary had been there. I was pretty upset about what happened. Even if you weren't my son, I would have been upset by what some members of our congregation were saying," he told Levi.

Levi felt a weight fall from his shoulders. "So you know, *Dat.*"

His father held his gaze and, in the older man's eyes, Levi saw sorrow and happiness and an overwhelming sense of pride.

"I know," Levi's *dat* murmured.

"I'm going to leave you two," Bishop Simon said, backing away. "I'll speak with you both before we meet for services again."

Levi waited for the bishop to go before speaking.

It actually gave him a moment to collect his thoughts and think on what he wanted to say because now that his father knew the truth, Levi's anger had fallen away. And he was glad of the release of that heavy burden. He was still trying to form the words in his head when his father beat him to it.

"I cannot tell you how sorry I am that I thought you had done something you had not, *Sohn*. I'm sorry I allowed doubt to overshadow what I knew of you, what I knew here." He laid his hand on his chest over his heart.

Emotion rose in Levi's throat. "It's *oll recht, Dat*."

"Ne," he argued, emotion thick in his throat. "It's *not*. When you called from the train station to say you had wed, I should have trusted you. When you arrived and I met Eve, I should have known there was more to your marriage than you were telling me." He bowed his head. "I should have just asked you."

Levi shook his head. "I wouldn't have told you. I had promised Eve."

His father smiled and sighed. "Ah, Eve. Our Eve. When Bishop Simon told me about her visit, I was as proud of her as I am of you, Levi." His voice caught in his throat and his eyes grew moist. "You married her for different reasons than we usually marry, but they were the right reasons."

Levi hesitated then, wondering if he should ask the question that was on the tip of his tongue. Or would it be better to let it go, because what did it matter now? It was over.

The words fell from Levi's mouth anyway. "If you suspected there was a reason why we married, why did you not support me Sunday when people were saying I shouldn't be considered? Why did you say God wouldn't choose me?"

"What?" His father stared at him, his bushy eyebrows knitting. "I never said God would not choose you. When did you think I said that?"

"I was standing nearby, *Dat*. You were all at John Fisher's fence."

His father hesitated for a moment, thinking. "I know what conversation you speak of, but I did not say God wouldn't choose you. I never said that because I've lived long enough not to assume I know God's ways. What I *said* that day was that we had to trust the process. I said that if God didn't want you to be a preacher, you wouldn't be chosen." He raised his hand and let it fall. "The reason I didn't just come out and say you should be one of the candidates was because some of those men might have assumed I was taking up for you because you were my son. Because I wanted you to a preacher so I could walk around telling people you were." He paused. "I never said you wouldn't be chosen because that wouldn't have been for me to say, *Sohn*. Only *Gott* could make that decision."

Levi exhaled, thinking back to that day. He had been so upset. Had his emotions clouded his senses? Had he heard wrong? He racked his brain and realized that now that his father had spoken those words, he couldn't *actually* remember his father saying differently. He pressed his hand to his forehead, pushing his hat back. Now he felt foolish. He had gotten himself so worked up about something that had never been said.

"You have a good woman there, you know," his father said. "She loves you so much. She would do anything for you."

Levi's head snapped up when he heard his father use the word love.

Eve loved him?

Where had his father gotten that idea? He was mistaken.

Wasn't he? She had certainly not said she loved him. But that didn't mean it wasn't true, did it?

"I can't believe I was so reckless in my thinking and my behavior." Levi's father was still talking. "I was shocked when you called to tell me you were married. And my first thought wasn't to believe you had taken liberties with Eve, but that there was a Godlier explanation. But then by the time you arrived, I'd had time to get myself worked up. I... I think that secretly I was angry that you didn't include me in your decision to marry. I was upset that you made the decision on your own. And I... I didn't get to decide for you. Or at least help you decide." He shook his head. "That makes no sense, does it? I raised you to be a good man, to make good decisions on your own, and then I was mad that you did?"

Levi smiled, realizing that an amazing calm was settling over him. His father knew now why he had married Eve, and he'd not had to break his promise to his wife. He exhaled and took a deep, cleansing breath. His mind shifted to thoughts of Eve, even as his father continued to talk. Levi wondered where she was. Up at the house, he hoped. Because he needed to talk to her. And he needed to talk to her now.

"Rosemary warned me I was getting myself worked

up without knowing the full story," his father went on, beginning to pace. "But I didn't listen to her. I—"

"Dat," Levi interrupted, stepping in front of his father. "I'm so thankful for your words, but I have to go. I have to find Eve. I have to thank her for going to Bishop Simon."

Levi's father smiled. *"Ya,* you should go. We can talk more later, *Sohn."*

Before Levi could turn away, his father wrapped his arms around Levi's shoulders and hugged him tightly. Then, without another word, he released him, and Levi went in search of his wife.

Levi looked for Eve in the kitchen, but no one was there and an illogical sense of panic flared in his chest. Where was his wife? Had she reached the limit of her patience with him and left him?

But where would she go? And after breakfast, she'd told him she'd see him for dinner. She'd made no plans to leave him or go anywhere. So she had to be there somewhere.

Levi found Tara feeding the chickens and she sent him to the garden. The short walk from the clothesline in the side yard to the garden in the back seemed to stretch for miles. Then, at last, he spotted Eve in a row of summer squash, filling her apron with the ripe yellow vegetables.

Levi thanked God under his breath and called out, "Eve!"

She glanced up, and seeing him, smiled hesitantly. As he approached, she looked uneasy, which he completely understood. Things had been going so well between them the last few weeks. They had been getting to know each other, and the better he knew his wife, the more he found he liked her. And she liked him. At least he *thought* she did. But then the business with choosing preachers had happened and Levi had become brooding the way he had been when they arrived, separating himself emotionally from her. Instead of cleaving to his wife as God wanted married couples to do, in the face of hardship, he had abandoned her.

And her response to his emotional abandonment had been to go to their bishop and confess to him the mistakes she had made. To protect Levi's reputation, she had sacrificed herself and possibly her own reputation. Why would she do that after the way he had treated her?

Levi's father's words pushed their way into his head: *She loves you so much.*

Did she love him? And if she did, would she forgive him for all the mistakes he had made since they wed?

Levi hurried down the path between a row of summer squash and zucchini. "I've been looking for you everywhere."

"You have?" She dropped the squash, one by one, from her dusty, oversize apron into a basket. "Why? Is everything all right?"

He walked up to her, taking her hands in his. "I hope so, Eve." He looked into her brown eyes that seemed, at this moment, to be the most beautiful eyes he had ever seen. He studied her round face, taking in the length of her eyelashes, the pink in her cheeks and the bowed shape of her mouth. He had the sudden urge to kiss her on her beautiful mouth.

But he didn't because, at this moment, he didn't feel he had the right to kiss her.

"Bishop Simon came to talk to me, and he told me what you did." He squeezed both of her hands in his. "I can't believe you told him everything. For me," he added, the words catching in his throat.

She nodded, her smile still hesitant. "I did."

"But why?" he asked.

Her brows knitted. "Because it was the right thing to do, Levi."

"But we agreed no one needed to know."

"I know we did, but, thinking back, I realized that decision was made in haste. It was a selfish choice. It didn't occur to me that you family, your community would question your motive for marrying me." She shook her head. "We should have told Benjamin and Rosemary as soon as we got here. And then, when your name came up as a candidate for preacher and folks questioned it, I knew I had to do something."

He drew his head back. "How did you know about that?"

"Tara."

He frowned.

"Don't be angry with her. She loves you and wants the best for you. She only told me because you didn't." Eve paused and then said firmly, "You should have told me about the men at church and what they said, Levi. You're my husband. You're supposed to tell me those kinds of things."

"I know, I know. You're right." He glanced up, squinting in the bright sunlight that was beating down on them. "You want to sit down for a minute? There's something else I want to tell you."

"Of course."

Levi led Eve by her hand out of the vegetable garden and into Rosemary's fenced-in herb garden. Along one side of the white picket fence was a small, oblong pond with cattails, miniature lily pads and a decorative rock border. A wrought-iron bench sat beside the pond under the shade of several pink flowering crepe myrtle trees. The pond had been there when they bought the farm from Englishers, Rosemary had told her. It was the little pond and the fenced-in herb garden that had sold her on the property as much as the amount of land and rambling white farmhouse.

"Let's sit over here," Levi told her.

Eve was so relieved that Levi wasn't angry with her about going to Bishop Simon that, for the first time since she'd spoken with Simon she actually felt as if she could breathe again. In celebration, she inhaled deeply.

At the bench, Levi waited for her to sit first and then he sat down beside her, and not on the other end, but right beside her. He took her hand again and she shifted, pleased and uncomfortable at the same time. Even if Levi had been angry about her going to the bishop, she knew it had been the right thing to do. But knowing her husband wasn't angry made her heart sing. But she was also concerned. What did he want to talk to her about?

Eve waited for what seemed like a long time, waiting for Levi to speak. She could tell by the look on his face that he wanted to say something, he just wasn't ready. To ease the tension, she asked him, "What did

Bishop Simon say about your name coming up for one of the new preachers?"

"He said that I would be one of the men to choose from the stack of hymnals the next time the congregation meets."

She looked up at him, thrilled by the feel of Levi's hand in hers and his undivided attention. "And what about what the men were saying about you?"

"Bishop Simon said he would tell anyone who brought the issue up that he had discussed with us why we married as we did and that he deemed me eligible to accept the job of preacher, should I be chosen. He said no one else ever need know."

Her palm feeling sweaty, she pulled her hand from his. "I think we need to tell Benjamin. If Rosemary hasn't already told him."

"The bishop told him." His voice broke with emotion, emotion Eve felt in her chest along with him. "And *Dat* came into the shop and talked to me after Simon."

"And everything is okay between you now?"

Levi smiled, his relief obvious. "It is."

"Oh, Levi," she sighed. "I'm happy for you. I know how your father's disappointment was weighing on your heart."

"*Dat* said he was sorry for being angry and disappointed with me. He also said he thinks I would make a good preacher." He shrugged. "If it's God's will."

"Of course you would be a good preacher!" she exclaimed. "I told Bishop Simon that."

"He told me," Levi said, sounding almost bashful.

"I think the faith you could show a congregation,

faith in scripture and in God's word, could do so much good here in Hickory Grove."

"I'm young for a preacher, though," he said.

"*Ya*, but I'm not sure that matters. And I bet your father thinks the same," she told him, happy beyond words for him. No matter what he said, she knew how upset he had been about the riff between him and his father. And that had upset her because she had been responsible for Benjamin's assumptions, if not directly, then indirectly.

"Oh, Levi. I'm so happy for you." Without thinking, she threw her arms around him, then, realizing what she had done, started to pull away.

But Levi held on to her and hugged her tightly. "I've been such a fool, Eve," he whispered in her ear. "I'm so sorry for my behavior toward you. God gave me a gift in you. He gave me a beautiful wife and I was so caught up in myself that it took me too long to see that." He leaned back so that he was looking into her eyes. "But I see it now. And…and I need to tell you that standing in my shop, listening to Bishop Simon and then to my father, I realized…"

He swallowed hard and glanced away.

"You realized what, Levi?" she whispered. "Tell me. You can tell me anything."

"I realized…" He met her gaze again and this time it didn't stray. "I realized that I've fallen in love with you, Eve. I don't know how." He shook his head. "Or when, but it's happened. I love you."

Eve didn't realize she had been holding her breath until it escaped in a great sigh. "You do?" Tears welled in her eyes.

"I do, and I don't care that you don't love me." He kept gazing into her eyes, talking faster than before as if he needed to get it all out at once. "I know that can only come in time, but—"

"Oh, Levi—"

"But I hope that someday you can love me," he went on, not seeming to have heard her. "I hope you can love me someday, if only half as much as I love you right now. I know it's a lot to ask but—"

"Levi," she interrupted and then she laughed when he finally fell silent. "I love you, too," she told him, her heart pounding in her chest.

He placed both of his hands on her cheeks and gazed into her eyes. "You do?"

She nodded, no longer even trying to fight her tears of joy. "I think I've loved you since that day in the barn when you saved me from Jemuel and my father."

They were both silent for a long time, lost in the moment, and then Levi got up off the bench. "Well, if you love me, and I love you, there's only one thing I can do." He reached for her hand.

"What's that, husband?" she asked, accepting his hand and coming to her feet. Behind her, she could hear the trickling water of the little waterfall in Rosemary's pond. The sun was warm on her face and there was a breeze carrying with it the scent of freshly cut grass and roses.

Levi faced her, taking her hand between his. "Eve, will you marry me?"

She blinked and then threw back her head in laughter, but also in joy. "Marry you?" she asked. "Levi, we're already married."

"We *are*?" he asked, sounding as if it were news to him.

Her laughter turned into giggles. "*Ya*, that's why I call you husband, and you call me wife."

"Is that so?" He moved even closer, wrapping his arms around her until they were so close that their noses were nearly touching.

"Ya," she giggled. "It's so."

"Huh." He looked away as if contemplating the truth of her words, then fixed his gaze on her again. "Then if we're already married, wife, I have another question for you."

The feel of Levi's arms around her, the scent of him so close, made her giddy. Her heart was singing, *He loves me! My Levi loves me!*

Her husband looked into her eyes again. "You want to hear my question?"

She nodded. "I do."

"May I kiss you?"

Eve's breath caught in her throat. "*Ya*, I would like that," she whispered.

For a long instant, Levi gazed into her eyes and then, slowly, he lowered his mouth to hers. She closed her eyes, recalling the first sweet kiss they had shared. But then, the kiss turned from one of innocence to a kiss meant to be between a man and his wife who were in love. And when Levi at last drew back, she gazed into his gray eyes.

"Wow," she whispered, knowing she was blushing.

"*Ya*, wow," he agreed.

She took in a ragged breath. "I should get back to

the house with the squash before Tara comes looking for me."

"And before I kiss you again, wife," he said huskily. "And again, and again."

She looked up at him through her lashes. "Maybe tonight?" she dared to suggest in a whisper.

"*Ya*, that I can promise," he answered, his voice still husky.

And then Levi took Eve's hand and together they walked toward the garden, knowing they were on the right path, at last, to a life of happiness and love.

Epilogue

One Year Later

Enjoying the feel of the warm grass beneath her bare feet, Eve pulled a wet towel from a laundry basket and tossed it over the clothesline. Next, she grabbed two clothespins from a blue gingham bag hanging in front of her. As she attached the towel to the line with the wooden pins and reached for another towel, she glanced at Rosemary, who was hanging little boys' denim britches and blue and green shirts.

"*Ach*, I'm sorry for all of this complaining," the woman who had become a second mother to Eve said. "At my age, it's hard to do things differently sometimes. You know that Benjamin and I have given our blessing for this marriage. It's not that I think it's wrong, only that it's not the path I saw a daughter of mine taking."

Eve smiled at her across the clotheslines as she scooped up a handful of washcloths and hung each one from a corner. The sun was shining and, while it was already in the eighties, there was a nice breeze coming out of the orchard, carrying the scent of apples from the trees. "You're not complaining, *Mam*, just telling me your concerns. Sometimes we need to say things out loud to settle them in our minds."

"Ya," Rosemary said with a sigh. "And to settle them in our hearts, as well." She looked up, past Eve, and lifted her chin. "Hmm, I think you have a visitor."

"A visitor?" Eve knitted her brows. "Now? Chloe said she wasn't coming for Tara and me until after dinner." The three women had a trip to Fifer's Orchard planned to get a couple baskets of the last of the sweet corn for the season. Their own sweet corn hadn't been as plentiful as it should have been because of a fungus early in the season, and they wanted to can at least another dozen quart jars for winter.

Rosemary's mouth twitched into a smile. "It's not Chloe."

Eve glanced over her shoulder and was surprised to see Levi walking toward her, grinning. He was wearing the blue shirt she had recently made him, a shade of blue that matched her favorite dress. He was smiling so broadly that she couldn't help but smile back and giggle with happiness. Seeing him between breakfast and supper had become a welcome surprise. He had been so busy all summer with new buggy orders that sometimes he packed a cold lunch, so he didn't have to stop working to trek up to the house for dinner. "What are you doing here? I thought you and Benjamin had business in Dover and then you were going to work on your sermon for Sunday."

As it turned out, it had been God's choice for Levi to be elected preacher of the new church district, and a fine one he was becoming. Her husband was still finding his way, speaking the words of God to the congregation, but every time he stood before them, her heart swelled with pride.

"The sermon can wait. And, *ya*, we did go to Dover." His grin seemed to get even bigger. "We had an appointment with a lawyer."

"A lawyer?" Eve drew back her head, glancing at Rosemary. She could tell, at once, that Rosemary knew what their men had been up to. But her mother-in-law wasn't going to be the one to tell her.

Eve returned her gaze to her handsome husband. "Why did you have to see a lawyer?" She felt comfortable asking because in the last year, she and Levi had worked hard to always be honest with each other and to tell each other everything.

"It's a surprise," he told her. "Rosemary, okay if I borrow my wife for a little while?"

"Of course. Go." She waved Eve away with her free hand. "This is the last of my basket." She clipped a wooden pin, attaching a little boy's peach-colored shirt to the clothesline. "I'll finish up the towels and see you later."

"Are you sure?" Eve asked, even as Levi was taking her hand to lead her away.

"Go," Rosemary assured her. "Enjoy a few minutes alone with your husband."

Eve looked up at Levi, still hesitating.

"If Rosemary says go, you go," he warned her.

Eve nodded and looked back to Rosemary. "I won't be long. I'll pick the rest of the grape tomatoes and bring them in when I get back. Tara wants to have cucumber tomato salad for supper."

"Take your time," Rosemary insisted with another wave as she picked up Eve's laundry basket.

Taking Eve by the hand, Levi led her across the back-yard.

"Where are we going?" Eve asked, tickled to have him to herself in the middle of the day.

"I told you. It's a surprise." He squeezed her hand. "How's Rosemary today?"

"Oh, she's fine. You know how she is. She just wants everything to be perfect for Bay's wedding. She wants it to be the same." She shrugged. "And it's not going to be like Lovey's and Ginger's. It can't be."

Levi sighed. "I understand." He smiled down at her. "You're good to be so patient with her." He cut his eyes at her. "And I'm sure that Bay will be forever grateful for your assistance in easing the tension."

She smiled up at him, her heart so full. In the last year, her whole world had changed so much. Not only had she gained a husband to love and be loved by, but she had gained an extended family that had welcomed her with open arms and a glad heart. "I'm thankful I can help."

Levi leaned down and kissed her cheek.

"Levi!" she murmured, pressing her fingertips to the place where he'd kissed her as she looked around to be sure no one had seen them. "Really. You're so naughty. Kissing me in broad daylight where anyone can see."

He shrugged. "There's no one around, but if there was, what would they say? 'Oh my, how terrible that

Levi loves his wife so much that he kisses her in broad daylight?'"

Eve giggled. "Tell me where we're going."

"The pond."

"The pond?" She made a face. "I don't have time to go fishing and I know you certainly don't."

He clasped her hand in his warm one. "We're not going fishing." Releasing her hand, he looked down at her, pretending to be irritated. "What makes you think I have time to fish in the middle of the day, Wife?" He waved both arms, speaking in a fake gruff voice. "I have work to do. Important work. *Man's* work."

She laughed, catching his hand and pulling it down. "Tell me why we're going to the pond," she begged.

"If I told you," he said, taking her hand in his again, "it won't be a surprise, will it?"

So, hand in hand, they took the path through the orchard and down the old dirt road that led to the pond. As they walked, they talked, though not about anything vastly important. Eve told him about the mouse she found in the pantry and the cheese and potato casserole recipe she was tweaking. Levi told her about a new order for a buggy and his concern that he was going to have to start a waiting list because he was worried about overcommitting himself and ultimately disappointing his customers.

They passed through a field of milkweed and wild black-eyed Susans, and the pond came into view. Eve stopped and glanced around. Nothing looked any different from how it had the previous week when they'd gone fishing on a Saturday afternoon. "Okay, we're here," she said, resting her hands on her hips. "Where's my surprise?"

"Just a little farther," Levi told her and together they walked past the pond and up a little bluff where weeds, saplings and grass grew.

"Here it is!" Levi declared, facing the pond, opening his arms wide.

She turned in a full circle looking for something, anything that looked different. But it all looked the same and she was beginning to think he was pulling her leg. "This is my surprise? A bunch of weeds?"

"*Ya*, well, no." His hand shot out and he grabbed her hand. "Careful, you don't want to walk into the wall."

Smiling, she looked at him suspiciously. "What wall?"

He moved to stand beside her and together they gazed at the pond in the distance. "This is the front wall of our house," he whispered in her ear.

Eve's jaw dropped and she looked up at her husband. "Our house," she breathed. "Here?" She looked out at the pond again. Dragonflies flew lazy circles around the cattails on one end, and there was a cacophony of frog and insect song.

He was smiling down on her. "Right here," he said softly. "If this is where you want to live. *Dat* and I went to the lawyer's today so he could give us this land. You and I now own fifteen acres, and they include the pond." He caught a wisp of hair at her temple and tucked it behind her ear. "If you don't like this view, we can find another spot." He pointed west. "We have woods over there, if you prefer that."

"Oh, Levi," she murmured, tearing up as she studied the pond, *their* pond. "This is perfect."

"I thought you would like it. Which was why I wanted to surprise you," he told her.

She nibbled on her bottom lip. "But I don't have a surprise for you."

He shook his head. "I don't need a surprise. All I need is you, Eve."

"Wait," she said suddenly. "On second thought, I do have a surprise for you. You might have to wait for it, though."

It was his turn to grin suspiciously. "And what am I waiting for?"

She took his hand and pressed it to her rounded belly. At five months pregnant, she was, at last, showing, which made her so happy. It was finally becoming real: her marriage, the love she and Levi shared, and now their baby.

Levi gently caressed her belly. "*Ya*, I know I'll have to wait on this, but this isn't exactly a surprise." His grin was wry. "I've known about our little one for months."

"But that's not your surprise," she told him, beginning to slowly move his hand to different places on her belly. "Try here." She pushed his hand a little harder and was rewarded with a response.

The movement so startled Levi that he pulled his hand away, staring at her swollen belly, covered by her favorite blue dress and an oversize white apron. "Is that…" He looked up at her and then at his hand on her abdomen, then back to his wife. "That's our baby?"

She teared up again. Everything these days made her cry. "*Ya*, our little *bobbel*, husband."

The baby gave another kick, and Levi inhaled sharply and looked down at Eve, his face full of wonder. "Our *bobbel*, Eve. We're going to have a baby."

She laughed, covering his hand with hers again. "*Ya*, I know, Levi." She lifted one foot, showing him a bare ankle. "And hot days like today, I've the swelling to prove it."

Smiling down at her, Levi slid his hand from her belly to wrap his arms around her and hug her tightly. "*Danke*, Eve."

She laughed and snuggled against his broad chest. "For what?"

"For marrying me. For forgiving me for all the mistakes I made the first months we were married. For loving me. For carrying our son or daughter."

She slid her arms around his neck, gazing up into his blue-gray eyes. "You're welcome."

"I love you, wife," he whispered in her ear.

Eve opened her eyes to gaze over his shoulder at the pond that would soon grace their front yard. "And I love you, husband."

And then she kissed him on the mouth in broad daylight and silently thanked God in heaven for Levi and his family and the love He blessed her with every day.

* * * * *

Dear Reader,

I hope you enjoyed Levi and Eve's story. I was worried they were never going to be able to make their marriage work, weren't you? I truly think that their faith in God and their belief in the sanctity of marriage is why they were able to persevere. Much like an arranged marriage, theirs had some unique challenges, but in the end, they found love and I'm so happy for them both.

Next, it's time for me to move on to a new challenge in Hickory Grove. Levi's stepsister Bay isn't even entirely sure she ever wants to marry. She's enjoying the freedom she has working full-time in her greenhouse too much. But what's going to happen when she meets Mennonite David Jansen? Will she change her mind about marriage? Will she be willing to leave the Amish church to wed him? Will David become Amish to make her his wife?

We'll just have to wait and find out, won't we?

Blessings,
Emma

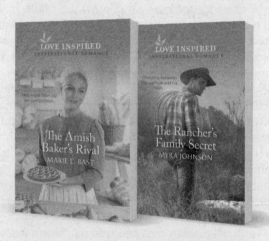

*When Susannah Peachy returns to her grandfather's
potato farm to help out after her grandmother is injured,
she's not ready to face Peter Lambright—the Amish
bachelor who broke her heart. But she doesn't know his
true reason for ending things…and it could make all the
difference for their future.*

Read on for a sneak peek at
An Unexpected Amish Harvest *by Carrie Lighte.*

"Time to get back to work," Marshall ordered, and the other men pushed their chairs back and started filing out the door.

"But, *Groossdaadi*, Peter's not done with his pie yet," Susannah pointed out. "And that's practically the main course of this meal."

Marshall glowered, but as he put his hat on, he told Peter, "We'll be in the north field."

"I'll be right out," Peter said, shoveling another bite into his mouth and triggering a coughing spasm.

"Take your time," Lydia told him once Marshall exited the house. "Sweet things are meant to be savored."

Susannah was still seated beside him and Peter thought he noticed her shake her head at her stepgrandmother, but maybe he'd imagined it. "This does taste *gut*," he agreed.

"*Jah*. But it's not as gut as the pies your *mamm* used to make," Susannah commented. "I mean, I really appreciate that Almeda made pies for us. But your *mamm*'s were extraordinarily *appendithlich*. Especially her *blohbier* pies."

"*Jah*. I remember that time you traded me your entire lunch for a second piece of her pie." Peter hadn't considered what he was disclosing until Susannah knocked her knee against his beneath the table. It was too late. Lydia's ears had already perked up.

"When was that?" she asked.

"It was on a *Sunndaag* last summer when some of us went on a picnic after *kurrich*," Susannah immediately said. Which was true, although "some of us" really meant "the two of us." Peter and Susannah had never picnicked with anyone else when they were courting; Sundays had been the only chance they had to be alone. Dorcas, the only person they'd told about their courtship, had frequently dropped off Susannah at the gorge, where Peter would be waiting for her.

"Ah, that's right. You and Dorcas loved going out to the gorge on *Sunndaag*," Lydia recalled. "I didn't realize you'd gone with a group."

Susannah started coughing into her napkin. Or was she trying not to laugh? Peter couldn't tell. *How could I have been so dumm as to blurt out something like that?* he lamented.

After Lydia excused herself, Peter mumbled quietly to Susannah, "Sorry about that. It just slipped out."

"It's okay. Sometimes things spring to my mind, too, and I say them without really thinking them through."

It felt strange to be sitting side by side with her, with no one else on the other side of the table. No one else in the room. It reminded Peter of when they'd sit on a rock by the creek in the gorge, dangling their feet into the water and chatting as they ate their sandwiches. And instead of pushing the romantic memory from his mind, Peter deliberately indulged it, lingering over his pie even though he knew Marshall would have something to say about his delay when he returned to the fields.

Susannah didn't seem in any hurry to get up, either. She was silent while he whittled his pie down to the last two bites. Then she asked, "How is your *mamm*? At the frolic, someone mentioned she's been…under the weather."

I'm sure they did, Peter thought, and instantly the nostalgic connection he felt with Susannah was replaced by insecurity about whatever rumors she'd heard about his mother. Peter could bear it if Marshall thought ill of him, but he didn't want Susannah to think his mother was lazy. "She's okay," he said and abruptly stood up, even as he was scooping the last bite of pie into his mouth. "I'd better get going or your *groossdaddi* won't let me take any more lunch breaks after this."

He'd only been half joking about Marshall, but Susannah replied, "Don't worry. Lydia would never let that happen." Standing, she caught his eye and added, "And neither would I."

Peering into her earnest golden-brown eyes, Peter was overcome with affection. *"Denki,"* he said and then forced himself to leave the house while his legs could still carry him out to the fields.

Don't miss
An Unexpected Amish Harvest *by Carrie Lighte,*
available September 2021 wherever
Love Inspired books and ebooks are sold.

LoveInspired.com

LIEXP0821